Illusions Of Magic
The MOVIE

J. B. Rivard &
Anya Carlson

Soft cover ISBN: 978-0-9968363-3-3
eBook ISBN: 978-0-9968363-2-6

Illustrations and cover design by J.B. Rivard

Interior design by Gray Dog Press
Printed in the United States of America
by Gray Dog Press, Spokane, Washington

Illusions of Magic

The Movie

by J. B. Rivard & Anya Carlson

What the Heck is This?

Illusions of Magic, a novel by one of us, was published in April, 2016. You may not have seen it on the New York Times Best Seller list, but readers seem to enjoy it. Some reviewers have given it raves. And some historians—apart from the more fussy academicians—give it good marks for faithful rendition of the history of the wounding and death of Chicago Mayor Anton Cermak.

But it has not been optioned, much less received the fabled 'green light,' to be made into a movie.

This is not to say the novel wouldn't make a good movie. One reviewer said, "You'll even imagine yourself seeing images flash across a movie screen in black and white as you read the book." Although it might make an interesting film, today's movie studios are off on a separate track.

In years past, studios made a wide variety of movies for a range of preferences, ages, and demographics. Now it's mostly mega-budget brand-name franchises, superheroes, toys, and filmed comic books. Twenty years ago, Robert McKee saw filmdom's "Weak stories, desperate to hold audience attention, degenerate into multimillion-dollar razzle-dazzle demo reels." As producer Lynda Obst recently wrote from Hollywood, "Movies are now an endangered species in the very place that makes them."

But wait. What if there were a 'What If?' What if, absent a silver screen, readers might experience the visual and aural effects of a movie version of *Illusions of Magic*? Below we describe the idea and its implementation. But first, some words about the screenplay itself.

The Screenplay

In the fall of 2016, we began developing a screenplay adaptation of the novel.

It's important to know that, although we are not professional screenwriters, we tried to avoid underestimating its difficulty. We read, or re-read, books on screenwriting, from William Goldman to Syd Field to David S. Cohen. We studied the great scripts, from *Casablanca* to *Chinatown,* from *The Shawshank Redemption* to *The Trip to Bountiful.* And back in the '90s, one of us sledgehammered through the challenges of this medium to produce a couple of mediocre screenplays. Still, as Robert Towne of *Chinatown* fame wrote, "It's rare…that anyone has an understanding of how disciplined a good script must be, and how much work goes into achieving that discipline."

Adding to the disciplinary requirements of the medium is the difficulty of adaptation. Movies are restricted to telling a story using only pictures and sound, and should only rarely exceed 90 minutes in length. A novel may contain 60,000 to 100,000 words, whereas a 110-page screenplay less than 30,000. Producer Gale Anne Hurd (*The Terminator*) says, "Adaptations pose the challenge of determining which material is relevant, and it's especially difficult—though often necessary—to lose compelling scenes and characters from the underlying source material." Thus cramming plot and subplots into such limited space and structure requires adroit trimming, deft transitions and imaginative substitutions. These restrictions mean we had to delete parts of the *Illusions* novel, formulate new scenes, and squeeze the plot into a narrower format. At the same time, the changes had to be formulated in ways that did not significantly alter the overall arc or sweep of the story.

Approximately a quarter of the scenes in our 110-page screenplay are new. For example, the assassination attempt on president-elect Roosevelt by Giuseppe Zangara, which in the novel is simply reported by one of the novel's characters, is a fully-dramatized scene in the screenplay. Other scenes, such as those in an Alderman's office, dramatize political or medical issues that were discussed but not dramatized in the novel. These deviations and other changes may surprise readers, but were implemented to clarify understanding of the novel's overall themes as implemented in the screenplay rendition.

The 'What If'

Movies, we know, are but a series of still pictures, or images, presented quickly, with sounds added. Ordinarily, we experience movies in a theater, on TV, or on one of our many electronic devices. However, temporarily disregarding the sound track, cinema is not the only way we experience images—we experience them in several forms.

One of the forms is in the "mind's eye:" visualization in the absence of an external, physical image. Almost everyone—except those afflicted with what's called "aphantasia"—experiences images in this way. The "mind's eye," although apparently a complicated mental activity, is closely related to normal vision. Neuroscientist Paul King explains: "In mental imagery, as with vision, what is being 'seen' is a partial model of the visual world that has been constructed by the brain."

By a somewhat analogous means, most of us can also 'hear' a voice that exists only in imagination.

A few years ago, Michigan State researcher Natalie Phillips teamed with neuroscientists at Stanford analyzing readers' experiences. She reported that, when reading in a focused and engaged manner, readers appear to place themselves within the story they are reading, making it seem very "real."

What if a means were available whereby a movie might be experienced through reading? Using a reader's "mind's eye," and aural imagining, we set out to provide the 'What If.' It would be formulated as a modification of the *Illusions of Magic* screenplay.

To produce this, we considered the first task to be that of providing a direct, uncluttered and easy-to-read text. It should be arranged on the page so as to allow readers' eyes to range smoothly throughout the narrative. This meant doing away with much of the jarring spatial arrangements typical of screenplays and reducing distracting features such as "all caps" instructions and headings. It meant voiding the spacing rules that place a screenplay's elements at various distances across the page, deleting scene and time-of-day headings, and eliminating various cues and instructions meant for both camera and sound technicians.

On the other hand, preserving the screenplay approach—setting out the actions and dialogue of each character distinctly and episodically—was essential if the central idea of reading the movie experience were to be maintained.

A second task was to provide description of settings (location and date) and time-of-day, to augment what is lost by deletion of the scene and time headings, and adding wordings to evoke a sense of the locale and time impacting characters' actions and feelings. It also seemed necessary to supplement the resulting bare dialogue and action descriptions with some prompts indicating emotional or other attributes of the characters' dialogue.

Specifically,

- We do away with screenplay's spacing rules that place elements (action, dialogue, character names, etc.) at differing distances from the left side of the page—a convention designed for the convenience of moviemakers but distracting for readers.

- We delete Scene Headings like "INT. APARTMENT – DAY," and "BEGIN FLASHBACK." Although these help filmmakers easily and quickly determine changes in setting and light conditions, readers find them abrupt, jarring, and cryptic. We substitute sentences describing each scene and/or shifts in time. A change of scene is denoted by an image of a top hat centered horizontally.

- We eliminate camera instructions, such as TRAVELING, P.O.V., CLOSE-UP, etc., including "BACK TO SCENE." We also omit sound effect notations such as "SOUND of gunshot," "tires SCREECHING," etc.", and sound technician aids "V.O., O.S.," as well as telephone filtering instructions.

- The identities of speaking characters are left-justified and printed in bold: **Steve.** Each speaker's dialogue is left-justified following the character's name. Each pair (speaker name and dialogue) is separated from other pairs and other elements by blank lines.

- Setting descriptions and characters' actions are *italicized* and separated from other pairs and elements by blank lines.

- Emotional and directional prompts are printed entirely in lower case, omit most punctuation, and are *italicized*.

- We subdivided the narrative into its three natural components, Act One, Act Two and Act Act Three.

We sincerely hope these modifications, together with the array of character identifiers and dialogue from the source screenplay, yield an easy-to-read narrative allowing readers' imagination to supply the visual and aural cues that simulate a "movie" experience. We call it "StoriVision," but other names would do as well.

Sources and Acknowledgements

The primary source for this book is *Illusions of Magic: Love and Intrigue in 1933 Chicago*, by J. B. Rivard. First published as an illustrated, historical novel April 17, 2016 on the Kindle eBook platform of Amazon.com (ISBN 978-0-9968363-1-9), it is currently available there. A print edition (ISBN 978-0-9968363-0-2) is also now generally available, online and in bookstores.

The secondary source is *Illusions of Magic*, the screenplay by J. B. Rivard and Anya Carlson, the second draft of which was finished in 2016. This screenplay is available to industry personnel from the authors (contact Anya Carlson: anyacarlson5@gmail.com).

Information about the author, the background of the novel's historical content, its illustrations, and other material, including the current blog, is at www.illusionsofmagic.com.

A short video derived from filmed scenes of novel themes may be viewed on www.illusionsofmagic.com as well as on other Internet video sites.

This book and these sources would not have appeared without the help and advice of many people; a few are named below.

Russel Davis of Spokane's Gray Dog Press is not only a fount of information on books and printing, he practices the intricacies of digital publication as well as traditional printing and publication. He is responsible for the great quality of our printed books, and has helped us in too many other ways to count.

Tim Chapman, President of Alt29 Design Group, took on the task of translating our ideas and plans for the book's website from drawing board to Internet reality. Together with artist/designer Mike Emenegger, he produced the visually-stunning, viewer-friendly, multipage, fast-loading website www.illusionsofmagic.com.

Sheldon Siegel, New York Times best-selling author of legal thrillers, took the time in 2002 to read J.B.'s fiction and give not only evaluation, but help and encouragement.

Dr. Willard M. Oliver, professor at Sam Houston State University and co-author of *Killing the President*, read *Illusions* in pre-release and wrote a positive review for publication.

Mel Ayton, author of *Hunting the President* and other books on presidential assassinations and attempts, read *Illusions* in pre-release and supplied a positive review for the book's initial appearance.

Blaise Picchi, author of *The Five Weeks of Giuseppe Zangara* (the attempted assassin of FDR) wrote a review that appeared on the back cover of the novel's first printing.

John Wilson, author and retired Dean and Professor at Golden Gate University School of Law, supplied a short review for the initial edition of the novel.

Wes Deitrick, producer and director, assembled the production team and actors who unerringly filmed the *Illusions of Magic* themes and edited the promotional video into being.

Neither the novel *Illusions of Magic* nor recent offshoots would have happened absent Anya Carlson's and Ivy Rivard's love for, and support of, the novel's author.

Act I

A movie theater marquee in Chicago, February, 1933. It reads "FRANKENSTEIN STARRING BORIS KARLOFF." Below in smaller letters "ALSO LIVE MAGIC".

Inside, on stage, professional magician Nick Zetner, forty-ish, performs. Beautiful wife Connie, his assistant, dances in a harem costume to Egyptian music.

Nick goes to a cabinet with a gauzy curtain over its open front, touches a switch. An inside light comes on, showing the cabinet is empty except for a fancy pillow.

Nick
to audience
As the lovely harem girl dances to the music, Seth the Malevolent Invader approaches.
exaggerated alarm
Quick! There is danger! The harem girl must hide!

Nick lifts curtain, Connie enters the cabinet, sits on the pillow. Nick drops the curtain. Connie can be seen behind the gauzy curtain.

Nick
There's a dagger in the Malevolent Invader's teeth! And the harem dancer can still be seen!

Nick turns the inside light out—now Connie can't be seen.

Nick

The darkness of nightfall hides the harem dancer from the Invader.

Nick steps away. A trumpet call is heard.

Nick

The trumpet call! In the nick of time, Basrah the Great has arrived!

Battle music is heard.

Nick

Will Basrah overcome the Malevolent Invader? Will he save the lovely harem Dancer?

The music grows louder.

Nick

The battle rages! But what of the harem dancer?

The music fades. Nick steps up, turns the cabinet light on, draws back the curtain. The cabinet is empty and the audience registers surprise.

Nick

The harem dancer is gone! Disappeared!

Nick begins turning the cabinet on its base, which permits rotation. The audience sees first one side, then the back— finally the opposite side.

Nick

The harem dancer is not here!

pause

Or here! She's nowhere to be seen! But that's impossible!

calling

Harem dancer! Where are you? Where?

Nick swings the front of the cabinet into view. The audience now sees Connie inside, sitting on the pillow. The audience gasps in surprise.

Nick

The harem dancer is not lost! She has reappeared! It's magic!

Nick steps away. Connie steps out of the cabinet and bows deeply. The audience applauds wildly.

Nick

Basrah has vanquished the Malevolent! The harem dancer is safe!

Egyptian music plays again as Connie smiles and begins dancing. A camera close-up reveals a gash across the back of her calf that is bleeding.

In Bayfront Park, Miami, on Feb. 15, 1933, a large crowd fills the park. They've gathered to see the new president-elect, Franklin D. Roosevelt. Floodlights pierce the night and highlight Roosevelt in his open limousine as he speaks into the microphone he's holding. Eager politicians press in around the car. Roosevelt sits atop the rear seat facing the crowd that enthusiastically greets his voice over the loudspeakers. He nears the end of his informal remarks . . .

Roosevelt
over loudspeakers
I hope that I am able to come down next winter, see you
all—

The crowd interrupts with applause and happy cheers.

Roosevelt
—and have another ten days or two weeks in Florida
waters.

*Roosevelt hands the mike to Miami's Mayor, flashes his
famous smile. The crowd applauds wildly. The drum and
bugle corps chimes in.*

Mayor
over loudspeakers, but weak
Thank you. Thank you—

The crowd's applause subsides a little.

Mayor
Thank you president-elect Roosevelt. I—

*Two shots interrupt the mayor. They come from a pistol
aimed at Roosevelt by a short, dark man near the front of
the crowd.*

Mayor
to Roosevelt
Get down!

*The assassin fires three more shots. Screams from the crowd
are heard. All five shots miss Roosevelt but hit people near
the limo. People in the crowd take the assassin down and
disarm him. Roosevelt's bodyguard leaps from front seat,*

covers the president-elect's chest. Secret Service agents rush to the rear of the limo, guns drawn. Screams, shouts and cries grow louder. The chief Secret Service agent pounds on the rear fender of the limousine.

Chief Agent
shouts to driver
Get him the hell out of here!

The driver starts the limo forward. Roosevelt strains to see the wounded people behind his car. A politician recognizes Chicago's mayor Cermak on his knees on the ground.

Politician
Cermak's been hit!

Two bystanders help Cermak to his feet. Blood begins to stain his right side above his belt.

Roosevelt
Stop the car! Get the—

His voice is drowned out by screams from the crowd. The limo stops. A Secret Service agent, gun drawn, looks back, sees Cermak.

Agent
Hey! That's the mayor of Chicago!

Roosevelt motions for them to put Cermak into the limo. Cermak crumples as agents and bystanders hoist him into the back seat next to Roosevelt. Roosevelt waves to the crowd.

Roosevelt
I'm all right. Tell them I'm all right.

In Chicago, Nick, still dressed as magician, unloads a box of magic gear from his car parked outside of their flat. Connie, in costume with her back against the passenger door, cocks her leg on the running board. She wears a scarf on her head and has pulled her bloused pant leg up over the knee. She holds a bloody handkerchief. Nick puts the box down amid traces of snow, stops and stares at Connie.

Nick
How'm I supposed to unload with you leaning on the door?

Connie glances at Nick, then dabs the gash on her calf with the handkerchief.

Nick
Well?

Connie
moving away
Well, yourself. It hasn't occurred to you it hurts?

Nick opens the door and tugs at the topmost cardboard box in the pile behind the seat.

Nick
I've reminded you before. You have to watch out when you—

Connie
Yeah, watch out. Like you always say, be nimble making the 'Vanishing Harem Dancer' vanish.

Nick
Yeah, nimble. And quick.

Connie
Sure. Be quick and nimble, twisting around in the dark.

Nick grips the box, lifts it, grunts. Connie moves in and helps wrestle the box out and onto the ground.

Nick
You complaining?

Connie
Twelve bucks? It barely buys groceries.
looks at him
We're not making it, Nick.

Nick
Things are changing. Look at the Edgewater Beach. Big bands, comedians, all the front-line entertainers. I'm telling you, we're going to be fine.

Nick resumes unloading boxes from the car.

Connie
The highfalutin Edgewater Beach Hotel is for big-time spenders. And with the Depression, where are people getting the money?

Connie steps back, dabs at her wound, winces.

Connie
They don't have it. They stay home, listen to Rudy Vallee, Ed Sullivan on the radio. For <u>free</u>!

Nick

Heck, in vaudeville, we worked three, four nights a week. Things have changed.

Connie

Have you noticed? There aren't any magic acts on the radio, Nick.

Nick circles the car, opens the passenger door.

Nick

The talkies cooked vaude's goose. Film's cheap. Run it over and over.

Connie

But people don't come to the Minerva to see our magic act, Nick. They come to see Frankenstein.

Nick

Okay, so people pay to see Hollywood stars, big names. But things'll pick up soon. The Depression won't last. Roosevelt's been elected. He'll get us moving.

Nick lifts a bag from behind the seat, carries it around. Connie looks at her bloody leg. She yanks the scarf from her head and hands it to Nick.

Connie

Can you tie this around my leg?

Nick kneels and wraps the wound. They resume unloading.

Nick

Look at Houdini! People still love magic—and Harry Blackstone, he packed 'em in at the Edgewater. Walt's trying to help us out.

Connie
With one booking a month at the Minerva? Nobody can live on one booking. And I won't be so beautiful in bandages if we don't—

Nick
I'll get that cabinet fixed so it doesn't… Listen, I've got a great idea for new patter on the sabers illusion.

Connie
There's nothing wrong with the 'Maiden Pierced by Seven Sabers,' Nick. Do you care if I'm hurt?
shivering
Do you care for the way we live? Do you care if I'm freezing here, trying to stop the bleeding?

Nick
preoccupied
It takes ideas. Maybe with bigger illusions, the act would be more spectacular…

Connie stops helping him and turns away.

Connie
That's the trouble, Nick. You're full of illusions about illusions. I'm tired of it, Nick. All of it.

Nick
now paying attention
Tired of the act, you mean.

Connie
facing him
No. All you do is dream of the Edgewater Beach Hotel! We're not going there. We're not going anywhere.

Nick
again distracted
I know it's been tough. It's a strain on both of us. But—

Connie
I just can't live this. This life.

Nick
looking at her
What do you expect?

Connie
You don't understand. I need a life. This isn't it.

Nick
You mean—you're not running out on me—

Connie
Actually…

A closeup shows a tear forming in Connie's eye.

Connie
I need—I need to be on my own, Nick.

Connie shivers, brushes the tear away.

Connie
now resolute
I'm going to live with Jack and Noddy.

Nick
To Liver Jack's? Jeez.
shaking his head
I—I don't understand.

Precinct captain Liver Jack sits in the alcove of his house at his roll-top desk. He holds the earpiece of a candlestick telephone snug to his ear. His cigar smolders in the ashtray.

Liver Jack
into phone
<u>What?</u> Can't be. Where? Okay, but what was—?

Astounded at what he hears, Liver Jack snatches his cigar from the ashtray, puffs furiously.

Liver Jack
That will sure light a fire. Okay, okay, I understand.

In the kitchen, Liver Jack's wife, Noddy, and Connie wash, wipe the breakfast dishes. They chat as Liver Jack enters and interrupts, waving his cigar.

Liver Jack
excited
You'll never believe! Cermak was shot!

Noddy
Oh my! The mayor! Is he—dead?

Connie
When? Where was he?

Liver Jack
He was down there in Miami, meeting with the butter and eggs man, Roosevelt.

Liver Jack returns the cigar to his mouth.

Liver Jack
Some Eye-talian tried to shoot him but missed, and hit the mayor. Some kind of socialist nut.

Connie
You mean the Italian is a socialist nut.

Liver Jack
For crying out loud, Sis. Isn't that what I just said?

Noddy
Is the mayor dead?

Liver Jack
He's critical. I don't wish him bad luck, but it don't look good.

Connie
to him
You made it sound like the mayor's a socialist nut.

Liver Jack waves the cigar at Connie.

Liver Jack
Aw, nuts.

Connie
And Roosevelt is not the butter and eggs man, Jack, he's the president-elect. As precinct captain, you should be more respectful.

Liver Jack, disgusted, jams cigar back in his mouth, puffs.

Noddy
Who was on the phone?

Liver Jack
Danny Hinkley. He called about that bank break-in, but couldn't shut up about the mayor—the shooting.

Liver Jack plucks the cigar out, points it towards Connie.

Liver Jack
to Connie
And you better hope Roosevelt's the butter and eggs man, Sis. The City needs every government dollar it can lay its hands on.

A telephone ringing is heard. Liver Jack dashes out of the kitchen.

Back in the alcove, Liver Jack talks on the telephone.

Liver Jack
into phone
Yeah, it's me.
pause
Yeah, I heard. I know.
another pause
What time? Yeah, I'll be there. 'Bye.

Liver Jack reenters the kitchen in deep thought. Noddy and Connie are still there, chatting.

Noddy
What'd Mr. Hinkley want—about the break-in?

Liver Jack
Huh? Oh. Wanted to know if I'd talked to Nick yet.

Connie
abruptly attentive
Nick? What about Nick?

Liver Jack
About a job, Sis. But never you mind. Thanks to you, Nick's on his own now.

Noddy
Now Jack! That's no way to—

Connie
Oh forget it, Noddy. Why would I expect my brother to understand?

Liver Jack
I understand one thing right now. Everything's on hold. There's a big ward pow-wow on what to do about the mayor and I've gotta go. Where's my hat?

In Miami, in a lab in the Jackson Memorial Hospital, two doctors stand at a light box that shows an x-ray of a man's torso. The lab doctor in a lab coat holds a manila folder while the surgeon, dressed for surgery, looks on.

Lab Doctor
This is patient—
consults folder
Uh, Anton Joseph Cermak—

Surgeon
Yeah. Mayor of Chicago.

The lab doctor closes the folder, places it on top of a file cabinet.

Lab Doctor
Oh? Really. Well, the bullet, a little hard to see—
points to x-ray
is here, close to the eleventh dorsal vertebra.

Surgeon
Oh, yeah, I see.
to lab doctor
No damage to the vertebra?

Lab Doctor
Well, I don't think so. The slug is anterior to the vertebra.

The surgeon turns to leave.

Surgeon
Okay. Get the x-rays to the East Wing. Thanks.

In Chicago, Danny Hinkley, dressed impeccably, strolls to the draped window of his luxurious apartment. On an antique settee, Nick sits holding his felt hat in his left hand. His right hand pulls the brim of the hat, slowly rotating it.

Nick
Liver Jack said you might have a job for me. In
connection with the break-in at the bank.

Hinkley
Uh-huh.

*His back still to Nick, Hinkley parts the drapes, glances
down at the roofs below, then turns.*

Hinkley
What'd you think of that?

Nick
I'll be frank, Mr. Hinkley. My business isn't hot these
days. The rent's overdue, and I'm—
stops the hat
Well, I'm broke.

Hinkley
I need a sharp, slick fellow for a certain job. But I don't
know you.

Nick
Liver Jack said—

Hinkley
Forget the precinct captain. I'm dealing with <u>you</u>. Why
should I hire you?

Nick
You're right. I'm just a guy off the street.

He grasps his hat by the crown, points with it.

Nick
Thousands more out there.

He stands, clamps the hat on his head at a rakish angle.

Nick
I'll be taking my leave, Mr. Hinkley.

Hinkley
in charge
Sit down, Mr. Zetner. You don't understand. You come highly spoken for, but I need to know more about you.

Nick
Like what?

Hinkley
Your past.

Nick slowly removes his hat, sits warily back onto the settee.

Nick
Sure.

Nick cocks one leg over the other, parks the hat on his knee.

Nick
Born here. Scraped through high school, got conscripted in eighteen to save France for the French. Back in the U.S., I might not have been real honest, but I didn't get arrested. Finally I decided to make a career out of dishonesty.

Hinkley
Dishonesty?

Nick
In high school I practiced sleight-of-hand, got
pretty good at it. So I took up magic—deception as
entertainment. Quite dishonest.

Hinkley
So you're a magician. But are you any good?

*Nick uncocks his leg, sets the hat aside. He raises his right
hand, shows both sides, reaches under the settee and brings
out a playing card.*

Nick
Good enough to wonder why you keep the ace of spades
under your settee.

*Hinkley smiles. Nick reaches under the settee with the other
hand and produces a lot of cards, which he fans for show.*

Hinkley
You're pretty good, Zetner. May I call you that?

Nick
pocketing the cards
Sure. What's this—job?

Hinkley
Those rapacious scoundrels that broke into my bank
that night—they emptied all the safety-deposit boxes,
including mine. They took money, documents, jewelry—
everything. Fortunately, insurance covers most of the
monetary loss.

Nick
It made the papers.

Hinkley
suddenly vulnerable
But I, I lost something—

Nick
A keepsake, a memento?

Hinkley
I'll pay <u>ten-thousand</u> dollars for its return.

Nick
skeptical, but nods
Uh-huh.

Hinkley
Ten thousand. For an envelope with its contents—some old snapshots.

Nick
You'd pay me ten thousand? Just for some snaps?

Hinkley
nods
Plus expenses.

Nick
pleased but hesitant
How would I recognize this—this envelope?

Hinkley
gesturing
It's manila, larger than a business envelope. It has thin purple stripes across it, and the flap is closed with sisal wound between cardboard buttons.

Nick

Even assuming I could find the— 'scoundrels'—what makes you think they'd give up the snaps?

Hinkley

Think about it, Zetner! These wretched heisters steal riches—jewels, money! What earthly use could such vermin have for nine snapshots? Snaps of people having fun?

Nick ponders this for a moment.

Nick

Well, if you're married, they might, uh—you have a wife?

Hinkley

Oh yes. My Martha is the spirit that lightens my day. The godsend of my life.

Nick

So blackmail is—

Hinkley

Think, Zetner, think! Can <u>you</u> be blackmailed?

Nick

Yeah. I see your point. How long do I have?

Hinkley removes a plain envelope from inside his suitcoat and hands it to Nick.

Hinkley

It may take awhile. I hope not. This will cover your expenses for now. Inside is a telephone number to use for contact. Other than that, you're on your own.

Nick stands, tucks the envelope away, picks up his hat and fingers the brim.

Nick
Just one more question, Mr. Hinkley. Those nine old snaps. Why didn't you get rid of them before?

Hinkley
Not that it's pertinent to your task, Zetner. Let's just say I enjoyed visiting with them from time to time.

The Miami courtroom is jammed with photographers, reporters, and newsreel cameras. The judge sits at an elevated desk. Down front sits the prisoner, Giuseppe Zangara, dark-skinned and small, about the size of a 12-year old. Also present are the Sheriff, prosecutors and deputies.

Judge
Mr. Zangara. Do you understand English?

Zangara
Yes.

Judge
Do you live here, in Miami?

Zangara
A little.

Judge
Do you know you are charged with four counts of attempted murder?

Zangara
Sure. They told me.

Judge
Do you want a lawyer?

Zangara
angrily
No—no lawyer!

Surprised, the Judge glances at the prosecutor, then at the Sheriff. He pencils notes on the documents before him, then looks at Zangara.

Judge
Because of the seriousness of this case, an attorney will be appointed to represent you.

Judge
I'm setting a date of Friday, February 17 for that.

Zangara's face contorts with anger. The judge picks up his documents and rises. The Bailiff announces "All rise." Zangara squirms in protest as three hulking deputies surround and almost carry him from the room.

Back in Chicago, Liver Jack slouches in his easy chair reading a newspaper. Noddy sits nearby crocheting. Connie, absent makeup and with hair wrapped in a towel, enters.

Connie
to him
So Nick's working for Danny Hinkley now?

Liver Jack
lowering the paper
Why should you care?

Connie
He's still my husband, Jack. And magic isn't making it.
He needs something that pays.

She goes to the mirror, fingers her plucked eyebrows.

Liver Jack
I wouldn't exactly call it paying. He's looking for those
mugs who broke into the bank. But—

Noddy
That article about the robbery said Mr. Hinkley was
going to make good on the losses.

Liver Jack
Glad I didn't have a box there.

Connie checks her neck for wrinkles, pauses to think.

Connie
Boxes. Something I heard the other day—

Noddy
Something about Mr. Hinkley's bank?

Connie
Might not be anything—

Liver Jack
curious, lowers the newspaper
Wait, Sis. Are you saying you know something about the
break-in?

Connie
Relax Sherlock. I'm not sure.

Liver Jack
intense
You know something, spit it out.

Connie
I don't spit, Jack. There <u>was</u> something.

With her eyes closed, she searches her memory.

Connie
Boxes, a haul—

Liver Jack
pressing
Something you heard? What was it?

Connie
glaring at him
Will you back off?

Liver Jack
defensively
It just might help Nick, y'know.

Connie
recalling
Something about boxes—'Artis,' that's his name. Plays clarinet at Lennie's.

Liver Jack
pleased
S'better than nothing. I'll tell Nick.

Liver Jack resumes looking at the paper. Connie unwraps the towel from her hair, rewraps it.

Connie
You know they say Mr. Hinkley paid <u>cold</u> <u>cash</u> for the bank. Can't be hurting for money.

Liver Jack
Might be made of money, but he sure is highfalutin. Talks funny.

Connie
Not everybody is as common as some of your friends, Jack. Hinkley's got class. Ran some big entertainment in New Jersey.

Liver Jack
So that's how he got the dough. Where in Jersey?

Connie
I don't know—Runrow?

Liver Jack puts the newspaper down.

Liver Jack
Runrow? Never heard of it.

Connie
Somebody said with the country on the way to repeal, Hinkley decided he'd quit Runrow.

Liver Jack bursts out laughing, nearly spits his cigar out.

Liver Jack
Chawww! I'll be a monkey's uncle!

Connie
scornful
Please don't include me among your simian relatives.

Noddy looks at him, lowers her crocheting to her lap.

Noddy
What's so funny?

Liver Jack
amused
You don't mean Runrow, Connie. It's <u>Rum</u> <u>Row</u>, the line of ships anchored out off the Jersey shore.

Noddy resumes crocheting.

Liver Jack
You hail a speedboat to get aboard, see? There's jazz bands, dancing, gobs of eats. But the main attraction is scotch, bourbon and gin, bottled booze by the case from Canada, Bermuda, wherever.

Connie tries to interrupt, but Liver Jack goes on.

Liver Jack
smiling
That's how fancy pants Hinkley made his big bucks.

Noddy
That doesn't sound funny.

Liver Jack
dryly
Just proves prohibition isn't good or evil—just profitable—that's all.

Connie
firmly (stressing "evil" in medieval)
Prohibition is 'mid-e-_evil_'!

Noddy
I still don't see what's funny.

In a hangar at an airfield near Chicago, a mechanic enters a small office. His coveralls, lettered "Midwest Aviation," are dirty with oil. Wiping his hands on a dirty rag, he speaks to an older man behind the counter. The older man wears baggy coveralls over a shirt and tie.

Mechanic
You wanted me?

Older Man
Yeah. Just got off the phone with Frank Jirka, in Springfield. His father-in-law is Mayor Cermak.

Mechanic
Down in Florida. Yeah, I read about the shooting—

Older Man
Jirka's a doctor, y'know. And he's got Dr. Meyer, head of County Hospital with him.

The mechanic nods, tentatively.

Older Man
Apparently, the mayor's chances are only fifty-fifty right now. Jirka wants me to fly him and Dr. Meyer down there.

35

Mechanic
In the Six-Thousand?
shakes his head
Not today. That oil regulator valve.

Older Man
Still?

Mechanic
shrugs
The replacement hasn't shown up.

Older Man
I see what you mean.
reaches for phone
I better call and tell them to try to charter out of Nashville.

In Chicago, Lennie's speakeasy is crowded this night. Windowless, it's dimly lit and smoky. A small band beats out a fast tempo on a narrow bandstand. Liver Jack, Connie and Nick sit at a table. The two men coax a reluctant Connie.

Connie
I can't talk to him while he's got a clarinet in his face.

Liver Jack
They're gonna take a break. Go over, tell him how great his playing is, invite him over.

Nick
Just like on stage. Use your charm.

Liver Jack
Use your hips.

Connie gives Liver Jack an annoyed look.

Later the band is on break. Connie is seen smiling and talking to a seated Artis holding his clarinet. After some back and forth Artis rests his clarinet on its stand and nods in agreement. He follows Connie to their table.

Artis sits at the table with Liver Jack, Connie and Nick talking about his past.

Artis
—started when I was nine. All I wanted to do was play trumpet. But instead I ended up with a battered clarinet.

Artis laughs, and the three join in.

Nick
to Artis
You heard about that robbery in Woodlawn? The Washington Park bank?

Artis
I heard. Why?

Nick
Oh, nothing. What do you drink? Can I buy you a shot?

Artis
Nah. I got my own.

Artis takes a flask from under his jacket, removes cap, takes a swig. Looks carefully at Nick.

Artis
Why'd you ask? You're not a cop, are you?

Nick
Oh no. This guy, friend of mine. He lost something in one of the boxes. It's not valuable, just kind of a souvenir.

Artis
Uh-huh.
takes another swig, smiles at Connie
You folks live around here?

Connie
I'm living—well, staying with my brother here.

Artis puts cap back on his flask.

Artis
Well, I'll have to be getting back.
to Nick
What's this souvenir thing?

Nick
Just an envelope. The stuff inside wouldn't mean anything to anybody.

Artis
You think your friend might pay for it? For the envelope?

Nick
Probably. I'd have to ask.

Artis stands, looks around, returns the flask to his jacket.

Artis
Gimme a number. A guy I know might get hold of you.

Nick scribbles a number on a paper napkin, tears off a piece and hands it to Artis.

Artis
Nice meeting you folks. Maybe I'll see you later.

Artis returns to the bandstand. Nick stands and gestures to Liver Jack that he's heading to the restroom.

Nick walks down the speakeasy's corridor. The door to the women's restroom opens and the beautiful Iris comes out, wearing an ankle-length gown with a V neck. She turns toward Nick and recognizes him. Nick, astounded, stops abruptly, stares at Iris without blinking for a few seconds.

Nick
Iris! What are you—

Iris
surprised but trying not to show it
Hello, Nick. I didn't think this would ever hap—but it has.

Iris shakes her head quickly, looks beyond Nick.

Iris
I can't talk now.

Nick
Wait. Where have you been? God, you look wonderf—

Iris
No, Nick. Please let me by.

She starts to pass him but stops short.

Iris
   nods toward the main room
I'm with someone—

Nick
Twenty years ago, I searched and searched—and now—

Iris
I know. I know, it's terribly unreasonable.
a tear starts in one eye
But I can't—<u>we</u> can't—

Nick scans around, then points to an alcove on the side of the corridor.

Nick
Quick. There. Over there.

Nick goes to the alcove, Iris reluctantly follows.

Iris
You don't understand.

Nick
Okay, then you explain. Where have—

Iris
impatient
There isn't time.

Nick
resolute
You don't remember Shabbona Woods? What we said that day?

Iris
Oh Nick, don't—don't you see I've got to go—

Nick
Okay, but at least give me a number. A number where I can reach you.

Iris
quickly
Oh no! You can't. But—
thinking, has an idea
Be at Harold and Ike's—on Sixty-third, Wednesday.

Nick
Wednesday. Harold and Ike's? Who are—

Iris
hurriedly
The butchers.' On Sixty-third.
She turns toward the main room.
I'll be there—around ten.

She passes him and hurries toward the main room. Nick follows for a short distance while mumbling.

Nick
to himself
Harold and—butchers. Sixty-third, Wednesday at ten.

Iris enters the main room. Nick watches her make her way to a table and seat herself next to a man with bronze hair. Now aware of his original goal, Nick turns back and enters the men's room.

Afterwards, Nick leaves the restroom and goes to the main room. He glances at the table where Iris and the man sat. The table is empty.

Nick and Connie Magic Show
(Patrick McHenry-Kroetch and Kris Crocker)

Directors Wes Deitrick and Jesse James Hennessy confer

Connie (Kris Crocker)

Director Wes Deitrick explains to crew

Author/Producer J. B. Rivard

Nick and Connie Magic Show
(Patrick McHenry-Kroetch, Kris Crocker)*

Hinkley (Wes Deitrick)*

Camera setup for stairs shot

Authors/Producers J. B. Rivard and
Anya Carlson with docile actor

Iris at speakeasy. (l. to r.) J. P. O'Shaughnessey,
Amy Sherman, Jason Jakober, Jason Young

Act II

In Miami, Giuseppe Zangara, unshaven, sits on a stool in jail. The Sheriff, surrounded by several lawyers and deputies, questions the prisoner. Zangara answers in a thick Italian accent.

Sheriff
When you talk to me, maybe I will go to court and tell the 'big judge'—

Zangara
interrupts
I don't care.

Sheriff
But I'll say Giuseppe Zangara said 'I want to kill president. I shoot the pistol.'

Zangara
I don't care—I am half-dead now. Capitalists, they make me this way.

Sheriff
Did you want to kill other people too?

Zangara
No. Just him. Just president.

Sheriff
What were you going to do? Walk away?

Zangara
No, no—

Sheriff
pressing
You wasn't scared—of all those people?

Zangara
No. What's the use of living? I'm half-dead now.

In Chicago, inside his flat, Nick slouches in a chair. At the sound of his landlady's voice, he jumps up.

Landlady
Zetner! Telephone!

Nick hurries to the landlady's, where he answers her phone. He hears a man's voice with a heavy Czech accent.

Krasek
Is Zetner? You?

Nick
Yes. Who's this?

Krasek
Know you Artis Greene?

Nick
Uh. Yeah, yeah. What's your name again?

Krasek
Call me Joe.

Nick
Okay, Joe.

Krasek
Pays money for—uh, thing? Yes?

Nick
Maybe.

Krasek
Meet, you and me? Huh?

Nick
A meeting. Sure. Where?

Krasek
Cicero. Rancoca's Billiards.

Nick
Rancoca's in Cicero. I'll find it. When?

Krasek
Past half-eleven. Okay?

Nick
How will I know you?

Krasek
Worry no. Find you, Joe Krasek.

In Cicero, tall windows flanking the door of Rancoca's Billiards are painted blue to exclude prying eyes. Nick enters the dark interior. Green felted tables are lit by shaded lamps hanging from the ceiling. Players include older men, some

with sleeve garters, and a few younger men. As Nick starts forward, his foot hits a tin pail of empty bottles, dumping it. Nearby players laugh at the clatter. Joe Krasek looks up, props his cue against the wall, and strolls toward Nick.

Nick
That you, Krasek?

Krasek
Joe. Joe Krasek.

Nick
Okay Joe.

Krasek gestures to a player at his table.

Krasek
Jiri. My shots. You take.
he stops short of Nick
You Zetner, eh? You a copper, are you?

Nick
No. No copper. I'm just trying—

Krasek
Your business, what?

Nick
I'm a magician. But lately—

Krasek
Magician. Do you circus, right?

Nick shakes his head 'no,' takes a cue ball from a vacant table.

Nick
I'll show you.

Nick displays the cue ball high in his left hand.

Nick
to everyone
What color is this ball?

Players halt play, laugh and say "white." Nick grasps the ball with his other hand.

Nick
Yes, it <u>looks</u> white. But when I stick it in this pocket—

Nick plunges ball into a pocket, yanks it back out. The ball is now the green #6 ball.

Nick
—the white ball changes color.

Players applaud. Nick quickly tosses the #6 ball to Krasek, who barely catches it.

Nick
Maybe it has only changed—pockets.

Nick shows his empty hands, digs a hand into a different pocket and lifts out a white cue ball. Players laugh and applaud.

Krasek
grins
In a pool hall many years, but never I seen jumping balls before.

Players laugh. Krasek signals for Nick to follow as he turns and heads for the front door.

Nick walks with Krasek out of Rancoca's and down a nearby alley. A light rain falls.

Krasek
For this thing. Pay you money?

Nick
Not me. Maybe the guy who wants the stuff.

Krasek
Eh, no good.

Nick
Look, I came here to deal. You don't want to deal, get me to the guy who will.

Nick and Krasek approach a dilapidated truck, parked in the alley. Crude letters on its side say "TRANSFER & STORAGE." Krasek climbs in driver's side, pats the passenger seat.

Krasek
Want a deal, huh? Sit.

Nick climbs out of the rain onto the tattered seat.

Nick
Nice truck.

Krasek
Go you to "Fourgon" cafe on Douglas. Order black beans and corn—

Nick
"Fourgon" cafe. I'll find it.

Krasek
Order black beans and corn syrup.

Nick
Corn <u>syrup</u>? You're kidding. Sounds terrible.

Krasek
intent
Order black beans and corn syrup.

Nick
catching on
Okay, okay. Order black beans and corn syrup.

Nick, in coat and hat, enters the Fourgon Café. It's a small room with a counter and a half-dozen tables covered in oilcloths. He approaches a waitress behind the lunch counter who jabs a menu at him.

Waitress
What'll it be?

Nick accepts the menu without reading.

Nick
Gimme black beans with corn syrup.

Waitress
Oh.

The waitress eyes the only other patron warily, an old man in a worn suit who sits at a table, busily eating.

Waitress
to Nick
I'll be right back.

She passes behind a partition. Amid a rattle of pans is heard the muffled voices of a man and woman. Soon, the waitress emerges.

Waitress
to Nick
This way.

She leads him into a corridor where she knocks on a door marked "Private." She nods her head toward the door.

Waitress
Go on in.

Nick enters a windowless room lit by a bare bulb. Seated at a small table facing him is Carney Sossek, smoking a cigarette. He offers Nick the sole extra chair.

Sossek
You're Zetner, eh? Have a seat. I'm Carney Sossek.

Nick tilts his hat back, ignores the invitation.

Nick
So I'm expected. Well, I don't go for all the cloak and dagger stuff. What's your game, Mr. Sossek?

On the table are pens, a phone and an ink bottle. Sossek gestures to an open bookkeeping journal.

Sossek
chuckles
Worry not. I don't do cloak and dagger. Just the books.

Nick
Both sets?

Sossek
ignores the taunt
Ah, you think there's a second cafe.
exhales smoke
No, just one. Why don't you have a seat?

Nick
sitting
Krasek must have told you why I'm—

Sossek
Of course.

Nick
How does Krasek fit into this, anyway?

Sossek
We're Czech. What do you want?

Nick
Krasek told you—I want to recover some snaps in an envelope.

Sossek
What're they worth?

Nick
Nothing. A guy just wants 'em back.

Sossek
You wouldn't be here if they weren't worth anything.
How much are we talking?

Nick
It depends.

Sossek pushes back his chair, knocks ash from his cigarette.

Sossek
grins
Look, Zetner. Everything depends. Finding that envelope
depends on how much it's worth.

Nick
grimly
Money. You want money. Up front, I suppose.

Sossek lifts a corner of the bookkeeping journal.

Sossek
As a favor, I keep the books for the owner of this cafe.
Sometimes he fixes me a nice meal.

Nick
archly
Black beans and corn syrup, I suppose.
stands up
Probably not. Okay. Nice meeting you, Sossek.

Sossek
rises from his chair
Wait. You walking out?

Nick

The guy might pay something for the return of the snaps.
But I don't have any money. S'long.

*Nick grips the crown of his hat, tips it toward Sossek, leaves
the room and the cafe.*

*Inside "Harold & Ike's Meats" on 63rd Street, lady shoppers
chat while waiting for service. On the counter are cured
meats, a roll of butcher paper on a cutter, a Toledo scale
with the emblem "No Springs". Behind the counter are two
butchers cutting meat. Nick, in coat and hat, enters, glances
around, hesitates, then returns outside where he waits,
glancing both ways down 63rd Street. Finally, after waiting
well past ten o'clock, he sees Iris in the distance hurrying
toward him. She's in a long coat and a felt hat, carrying her
purse.*

Nick

I thought you weren't—

Iris
a little breathless
I know. I'm late.

*Iris grasps the handle of the butchers' door to open it. Nick
puts his hand on hers, preventing its opening.*

Iris
I've got to get some salami and—

Nick
No. Please, let's go across the street—where we can talk.

Iris pauses, looks into Nick's eyes, slowly withdraws her hand. They cross 63rd Street, dodging traffic.

In a brightly-lit restaurant, two men on pedestal stools eat at a counter beneath a Coca Cola sign. A waitress behind stacks tableware. Nick and Iris, on wood chairs at a small wood table are served coffee by the waitress.

Waitress
Is that all?

Nick nods yes, looks at Iris. She smiles at the waitress.

Iris
to waitress
Yes, thank you.

The waitress leaves.

Nick
eagerly
This is impossible. After all these years—

Iris
tentative
I—I really don't know what to say.

Nick
You could start by telling me where you've been for twenty years.

Iris
shakes her head
I thought this would be easy—but it's—it's complicated.

bites her lip, stares at her coffee
I don't think I can go through with this.

Nick
Then why did you tell me to meet you? Today, at the butchers'?

Iris
looks at him
It's very unfair, I know. I thought I could explain everything. But now . . .

Nick
Is it that man? The man you were with?

Iris
slowly
Yes. And no. It's a long story, Nick.

She fumbles with the purse in her lap.

Iris
Too long. And too complicated.

Nick
He's your husband? I think I deserve to know.

Iris sets her purse on the top of the table.

Iris
No, he's not my husband, but—
grasps the purse, turns in her chair
I must go.

Iris stands, steps toward the door.

Nick
imploring
We can't just leave it there.

Iris pauses at table's edge. Nick pulls a pencil stub from his pocket. He writes a number on a scrap of paper, hands it to her.

Nick
It's the landlady's. Just ask for 'Nick.'

Iris
I'll try, Nick, but—

She places the paper in her purse. Nick takes her hand in his hand, tenderly.

Nick
Do you remember Shabbona Woods, before you went off to school? You said—

Iris
I said, 'I love you, Nick.' It was true—when we were eighteen.

She clasps her free hand on his hand that holds hers, then looks into his eyes.

Iris
It's still true.

Iris slips her hands free, turns and leaves without looking back. Nick watches her through the windows as she crosses 63rd Street and enters the butcher shop.

A little later, Nick has finished his coffee. He pays the bill and continues to look through the windows. He sees Iris leave the butcher shop carrying a package. She turns and walks briskly on toward S. Rhodes Avenue. He leaves the restaurant and walks along his side of the street maintaining visual contact with Iris walking on the opposite side. Iris is unaware he is following her. She turns left onto S. Rhodes Avenue and disappears from his view.

Nick crosses 63rd Street and hurries to the corner of S. Rhodes Avenue where he sees Iris walking on S. Rhodes. He follows, trailing her as she walks ahead of him on the opposite side of the street. Finally she slows, turns and ascends the porch and enters a gray clapboard two-story house with an outside brick chimney laced with a myriad of dead vines. He stops, stares at the house, turns around and walks back toward 63rd Street.

Later, Nick climbs behind the wheel of his car parked near the butchers' shop. It pulls from the curb and moves off. It passes the butchers' on 63rd Street, turns onto S. Rhodes Avenue and continues. Near the gray clapboard house with the chimney laced with dead vines that Iris entered earlier, it slows. Parked in front of the house is a shiny Oldsmobile sedan, facing the same direction Nick is traveling.

As Nick's car gets nearer, a man exits out the front door, descends from the porch and strides to the parked Oldsmobile. The man, hatless in a trench coat, gets behind the wheel. He does not seem to notice the approach of Nick's car. Nick glances in his rear-view mirror as his car passes the parked car. The man in the Olsmobile is Carney Sossek! Nick continues to watch in his rear-view mirror as the house and the parked car recede into the distance behind Nick's (moving) car.

Finally the Oldsmobile pulls from the curb and begins following Nick's car, a fair distance behind. Upon entering an intersection, Nick turns right onto a cross street. Sossek's Oldsmobile then passes the same intersection and continues travel on S. Rhodes Avenue.

In Miami's Jackson Memorial Hospital, in Mayor Cermak's wing, a small room is reserved for newsmen. Reporters from across the U.S. sit and type or talk amid tables, chairs, typewriters, and telephones. Bennie, a Chicago man newly quartered in Miami, sits at a table. He hangs up the telephone in front of him. Across the table a reporter scribbles in a notebook.

Bennie
irritated
Crap.

Reporter
looks up at Bennie
Problem?

Bennie
Ah, damn phone. I'm s'posed t'keep the boss informed. But Chicago don't answer.

Reporter
Chicago, eh? Which paper?

Bennie
shielding mouth with his hand
Nah. That ain't it. I'm here t'keep track on the mayor for Alderman Emrin.

Reporter
Oh. Well, these long-distance lines aren't very reliable.

Bennie
You're telling me! And right as the President calls to check how Mayor Cermak's doin'.

Reporter
President-elect.

Bennie
Huh?

Reporter
Roosevelt. He's president-elect.

Bennie
Oh sure.

The reporter returns to his scribbling.

Bennie
interrupts
You think we'll get the lowdown when this here Dr. Tice gives his report?

Reporter
Don't know. They've been in there for over an hour. It may be difficult to get six doctors to agree.

Bennie
Hell if I care if they agree or not. Just tell me if he's gonna live or die.

In Chicago, Nick plods the shadowed Plaza of White City Amusement Park. Only a few patrons linger. Nick's bundled up against the cold. Behind him are bright lights, carnival rides and a penny arcade. He anxiously looks all around and consults his pocket watch. He rubs his hands together to warm them. Shortly, Sossek arrives in overcoat and hat. Nick approaches him, but Sossek turns away and strides out onto the 63rd Street sidewalk. Nick catches up to him.

Nick
What? Where you going?

Sossek looks straight ahead, walks, does not reply.

Nick
Look. On the phone you said eight o'clock. I'm here for half an hour—

Sossek keeps going, Nick keeps up with him.

Nick
Where you going, anyway?

Sossek
dryly
This is a private parley.

Nick
gestures
So? There's nobody here. What are we doing? You got the material?

Sidewalk is empty of pedestrians. Sossek stops at a cross street, faces Nick.

Sossek
You think I'm dumb?

A car goes by.

Nick
You said—

Sossek
I said I found it.

Sossek crosses the cross street, resumes walking.

Sossek
I ain't dumb enough to bring it here.

Nick
Then what're we doing? And where—

Sossek
slowly, with disdain
Terms, Zetner. Terms.

A train roars overhead on the 'L,' wheels screeching. Both men look up, then Sossek leans against a support column. Nick stands several feet away.

Nick
I thought you had the envelope.

Sossek
restraining himself
We gotta agree on price.

Nick
Like I said before—

Sossek
insulted
Zetner, you are <u>thick</u>. We'll start at a thousand.

Nick
What?

Sossek
gestures
I gotta pay for this. You think this is easy?

Nick
I don't think the man will go that high.

Sossek
dismissive
A thousand clams or your man can forget his stuff.

Nick
I'll talk to him. But I don't think—

Sossek
You do that, Zetner. You tell him.
spits on the sidewalk
I'll phone you in two days.

Sossek turns, tramps down the street. Nick stands there, thinking.

Inside Nick's landlady's flat, she hands Nick her telephone.

Landlady
irritated

I'm really tired of these calls, Nick. You gotta get your phone back.

Nick
It's fixed. I paid the bill. But they gave me Franklin-seven-five-six-two-two.
into phone
Hello?

Iris
on the phone, softly
Nick, this is Iris.

Nick
to landlady
Now nobody knows my number.
into phone
That was my landlady. I finally got my phone hooked up. Why are you whispering?

Iris
There's somebody here—you understand? You know Star's?

Nick
Stars? I can barely hear you.

Iris
I can't talk loud. "Star Dry Goods."

Nick
Oh, I get it. Star's. Sure.

Iris
Meet me there. In a half-hour.

Iris, in coat and hat, stands outside the entrance to "Star Dry Goods." She smiles as Nick walks up.

Nick
Wow, I'm glad to see you're here. I could barely hear, on the phone.

Iris
I need to explain. See, it wasn't fair, the way I treated you at the cafe. I couldn't—

She pauses, can't find the words.

Iris
Oh why do I have so much trouble explaining?

Nick
You're out shopping. Is that it?

Iris
smiles
Yeah. "Fels Naptha."

On the sidewalk behind Iris, a young bicyclist approaches. Neither Iris nor Nick are aware.

Nick
"Fels Naptha?" Oh—

Iris
The laundry soap.

Nick and Iris laugh, nervously. As the bicyclist nears them, Iris unknowingly backs into its path. Nick sees the impending collision, grabs Iris, pulls her to him out of the bicyclist's path.

Iris
What was that?

Nick
holding her close
Wow! That was close!

Iris
now seeing the bicyclist
Oh my gosh! I had no idea—

Nick
smiles, enjoying the embrace
It seems like forever.

Iris
smiles
Almost twenty years.

Suddenly self-conscious, he relaxes the embrace.

Nick
You were saying—?

Iris
laughs
I forget.

Nick
laughs too
Something about "Fels Naptha."

Now inside "Star Dry Goods," Iris picks out the 'Fels Naptha Soap Chips' from among the 'O.K. Soap,' 'Duz,' and other brands on the shelf. Nick watches as she pays the clerk. They leave the store.

Nick stands outside the entrance to "Star Dry Goods," talking to Iris, who carries the box of soap chips.

Iris
—I've been with him for a long time.

Nick
Drives a fancy Oldsmobile sedan?

Iris
No—that's not him. "Red"'s his name. He's—

Iris looks down, then back at Nick.

Iris
embarrassed
He's not a nice man.

Nick
You said you're not married. Why not leave him?

Iris
slowly, reluctantly
I can't. It's complicated, I—

Nick
You know I went to Carbondale. To the college. To find you.

Iris
You mean—back then?

Nick
nods
All my letters came back, marked 'Return to sender.' So I went to "Old Main," to the Registrar's Office there.

The box of soap chips drops to the sidewalk. Iris's hands fly to cover her face.

Iris
Oh no!

Nick
The lady there was kind enough to tell me what was written on your enrollment card.

Hands covering her face, Iris sniffles.

Nick
It said 'Student not attending.'

He stoops to pick up the soap. She drops her hands, looks at him.

Iris
cries
You had no way of knowing. Oh Nick—

Nick sees her distress, tucks the soap chips under his arm.

Iris

I'm so sorry. You went all that way from Chicago—

She shudders, breaking down. Nick grasps her shoulders, tries to comfort her.

Iris
overcome
—for nothing. For nothing!

Nick
tenderly
Jeez. I didn't mean to upset you—

She cries, her words hard to make out.

Iris
It's all my fault—my fault.

In the reporters' room in the Miami hospital, Bennie is on the phone with Alderman Emrin in Chicago. He reads from a paper he's holding.

Bennie
into phone
'Mayor Cermak has maintained the gain made as a result of the blood transfusion. He is sleeping after having taken his first nourishment in the past twenty-four hours.'

In Chicago, Alderman Emrin, at his office desk, talks to Bennie.

Emrin
into phone
Uh-huh.

In an adjacent armchair is Alderman Ferozi, who listens to Emrin's side of the conversation.

Bennie
to Emrin
Do you want his temperature, pulse and restoration?

Emrin
No. I can't tell nothing from . . . did you say 'restoration'?

Bennie
Yeah. Like ninety-nine decimal four, one-hundred and—

Emrin
frustrated
Never mind. Those numbers mean nothing to me. Okay, he eats, he sleeps.

He gives Ferozi an annoyed look.

Emrin
Anything from Doctor Jirka, the mayor's son-in-law?

Bennie
While ago he said he considers the mayor to have little chance to live.

Emrin
disbelief
You sure? Frank Jirka said that?

Ferozi leans in, senses there's news.

Bennie
unemotional
That's what he said.

Emrin
Listen, Bennie. Find out what's going on with the mayor. And get back to me right away. You get me?

Bennie
It ain't easy. I'll do what I can.

Emrin hangs up, turns to Ferozi.

Emrin
Jirka says the mayor's a goner.

Ferozi gets out of his chair.

Ferozi
I better get hold of Pat.

Emrin rises from his chair, holds up a hand.

Emrin
Wait a minute. I know you think three men running the city is done for. But before we go off half-cocked, I think we better—

Ferozi shakes a finger at Emrin.
Ferozi
I'll tell you one thing. The town has never accepted the 'unholy triumvirate.'

Emrin
returns to his seat
I still think we better get Straxton in here.

Ferozi
dismissively
Aw—who says lawyers know how this city should run?

Ferozi draws a cigar from his inside pocket, sticks it in his mouth.

Ferozi
What else did Bennie say?

Emrin
Nothing. Bennie can't blow his nose without help.
getting to his feet again
I'm going to get Straxton.

Emrin heads for the door. Ferozi lights his cigar, watches Emrin leave the office.

Later, Emrin is back behind his desk. Ferozi is in his armchair. Straxton holds forth in an armless chair near Emrin's desk.

Straxton
I'm telling you, even if you could call the election, a minimum of a hundred and four days has to elapse before the election can take place.

Ferozi
plucks cigar from his mouth
That's not what I'm talking about.

Straxton
ignoring Ferozi's comment

The council has no power to elect a mayor pro-tem. <u>None</u>.

Emrin
gestures to Straxton
I thought we'd agreed that, if the mayor dies, you'd serve as mayor.

Ferozi
We aren't there. <u>Yet.</u>
Ferozi inspects his cigar's ash.

Ferozi
The whole thing's a—a whatchamacallit.

Straxton
nods
Ad hocism. It's extra-legal.

Ferozi gets up, grins, knocks his cigar ash into the ashtray on the desk.

Ferozi
Exactly. I'll take my 'legal' any way I can get it.

Emrin
We're off the track here.
to Ferozi
Don't forget that Bowler is backing Clark.

Ferozi
sits down
Yeah, yeah, I know. Then there's Doyle and Arvey. The question is, can we select a pro-tem mayor from among them—

Straxton
distressed, leans forward
You two are avoiding the point. The council has no
power—

Ferozi
We got the point. I'm just telling you—Pat knows how
to do this.

Emrin, impatient with the wrangling, slaps his desk.

Emrin
I'm telling both of you—we're going to call a meeting
of the Central Committee. We'll get together at the
Morrison and hash this out like good and faithful
Democrats.

*Iris crosses the porch of the house on S. Rhodes Ave., fumbles
to open the front door with a paper bag of groceries in her
arms. As she enters, a lanky teenager, Steve, approaches her.*

Steve
Mom, stay right here.

Iris
What's the matter?

Steve
Carney's dead. We're taking him to Indiana.

Iris
What?!
panicky, sets groceries down
What happened?

Steve
I was upstairs—I heard them arguing. Something about money.

Iris
You mean—

Steve
Then there was a fight, and—

Red, mid-forties, bruised, shirttail out, charges into the room.

Red
to Steve
Shut up! I'll handle this.

Iris
to Red
Is that right? Is Mr. Sossek—

Red
Never mind. He's dead.

Iris breaks down, begins to cry. Red grabs Steve by the arm.

Red
to Steve
C'mon. We got work—

Red and Steve exit the room.

A few minutes later, Iris looks through the kitchen window. She sees Sossek's Oldsmobile parked in the driveway on the side of the house. Red and Steve maneuver a heavy, rolled-up carpet into the rear of the sedan. They struggle with the weight. The carpet slips open, and part of a limp leg with a shoe on it protrudes.

Nick arrives at the entrance to his flat and unlocks the door. The telephone inside rings, and he dashes inside to answer.

Nick
Hello?

Iris
on phone
Nick! Something terrible's happened! Mr. Sossek's dead!

Nick
What? What happened?

Iris
They just left! In Sossek's car!

Nick
Who?

Iris
Red's driving. They're going to Indiana with Mr. Sossek in back—

Nick
Wait. I'm confused. What happened to Sossek?

Iris
Red—I think Red killed him. I'm scared, Nick.

Nick
Where are you now?

Iris

At home. The house on South Rhodes. Nick, I think the neighbors heard something. They're out front and—

Nick

The neighbors? Not good.

Iris

What should I do?

Nick

Can you—

Iris

I'm scared to death—

Nick

Can you get out the back, to the alley? Without the neighbors seeing?

Iris

Yes. Yes.

Nick

Go to the alley. Walk—don't run—south to Sixty-seventh Street. I'll pick you up there. Do you understand?

Iris

Yes, Nick. Yes.

A few minutes later, as Nick drives 67th Street, he spots Iris at the alley. Her hair is mussed, her coat unbuttoned. But she doesn't know Nick's car. He stops near Iris, rolls down the passenger-side window, and yells.

Nick
Iris! Here! Iris!

She dashes to his car and gets in.

Iris
Oh, Nick! Thank you.

As he pulls away from the alleyway, they hear the sound of a distant siren.

Iris
The police. Could they be coming?

Nick scans the street's traffic but sees no police car.

Nick
driving
Hard to tell. I'm gonna get off the street. Then you can tell me what happened.

Nick drives to a nearby cemetery where he parks on an interior road. Iris, in the passenger's seat, talks to Nick, who sits behind the steering wheel.

Iris
Mr. Sossek must have showed up after I went to the market. I've never dealt with him much—he's—he was a friend of Red's.

Nick
They had some kind of fight?

Iris
Uh-huh. When I got back Steve said, 'Carney's dead.'

Nick
Steve?

Iris looks blankly at Nick.

Iris
Oh God! I—I haven't. No, you don't—

Nick
Don't what?

Iris
embarrassed
Steve's my son, Nick. I'm sorry I haven't—please forgive me.

Nick
frowns
Let me get this straight. You live there with Red, and Steve is—

Iris
quietly
Steve's our son. He'll turn nineteen this year.

Nick hesitates, opens his car door, steps out, gazes around.

Nick
Jeez!

Iris
I should have told you before.

Nick closes the door part way, looks hard at Iris.

Nick
Uh-huh.

Nick goes to a nearby tombstone, sits on it, stares at the ground. Iris gets out of the car, comes around to face him.

Iris
shaking head
I know. I'm so sorry. I should have—

She turns, steps back toward car.

Iris
murmurs
Oh God. What have I done?

She turns back to Nick.

Iris
firmly
Just take me back, Nick.

Nick looks up, then at Iris.

Nick
Back? What d'you mean?

Iris
Take me back to the house. I deserve whatever happens. Here I am, messing up your life. Again.

Nick gets up and goes to Iris, grasps her shoulders.

Nick

Are you crazy? I love you—I'm trying to help. You can't go back there—

Iris breaks away, goes to a nearby tombstone.

Iris

I know you're trying to help, but I've been so terrible—I wanted to tell you, but—

Nick

It's just such a—How could I know you left college because you were expecting?

Iris

That's not it. That's not even half the story. No, Nick. I owe you the full story.

Iris plods to the car, opens the passenger's door, finally turns toward Nick.

Iris

Right after I arrived at school, several of us girls went to a roadhouse near Carbondale. It was a lark, really—we were underage and shouldn't have been there.

Iris continues her story . . .

Iris

We talked and joked with some of the men.

. . . as it unfolds in 1913 at a roadhouse near Carbondale. The interior is crowded, including coal miners dressed in

work garb. Freshman girls from the college, including a young Iris, mix in high spirits with patrons at a table.

Later, two miners argue at the bar. A third tries to intervene, which starts a brawl. Others join, provoking a spreading fight. We hear scuffles, grunts, and cursing. A man at the girls' table jumps up to join the fight. His feet tangle with Iris's chair, dumping her on the floor.

With his back to Iris, another man draws a knife to defend himself. But he's knocked over backwards, where he falls onto Iris. Unintentionally, he stabs her soft flesh midway up her thigh.

She grabs her thigh and screams, but it's lost in the general pandemonium. Not realizing he stabbed her, the man scrambles to his feet and rejoins the fray.

Blood begins to stain Iris's dress as she tries to get off the floor. However, a mid-twenties man at the girl's table, a young Red, sees her trauma and rushes to help.

Young Red
You're hurt. Here!

He muscles Iris up off the floor.

Young Red
Quick! This way! We gotta get out of here!

He tries to guide her away. She limps a step, then halts.

Young Iris
No, no! I can't! I can't leave my friends!

In pain, she grips her thigh and crumples into Red.

Young Iris
Oh God—this is terrible!

Young Red
Grab hold! We gotta get out of here.
He half-drags, half-carries Iris away from the melee and out into the night. Once they reach his parked car, he heaves a woozy Iris onto the passenger seat. He strips off his shirt, ties it around her bleeding thigh, and closes the door.

In the parking lot, young Red is behind the wheel with the motor running. He turns toward the passenger seat, where Iris holds her wrapped-up thigh.

Young Red
You're from the college, eh?

Iris nods. In the dim light, Red squints at her thigh.

It's not too bad. You'll be all right.

Young Iris
Yeah. It doesn't feel like it, though.

Young Red
looks around
We gotta get out of here.

Young Iris
Why?

Young Red
Sheriff'll be here right quick. And you're too young to be legal.

90

The camera pulls back to reveal the roadhouse and its parking lot. The headlights on Red's car come on and it leaves the lot. Just then, the Sheriff's car speeds toward the roadhouse on the main road, its siren wailing.

We return to the cemetery in 1933. Iris stands next to the open door of Nick's car and continues her story.

Iris
He—Red Nedders—took me to his house, cleaned and dressed the wound. He washed the blood out of my clothes. I stayed with him that night. Next day I told him I had to get back to campus. He took me, I went to my dorm. They hadn't missed me. I limped to some of my classes that week.

Nick stands by a tombstone, listening.

Iris
looks away from Nick
He came every night and brought food. The wound began to heal. He was good to me so I stayed with him the next weekend. Later, I found out I was expecting.

Nick, who trudges toward driver's side of the car, stops.

Nick
hesitant
I don't know what to say.

Iris
I was terrified.

Nick trudges toward the driver's side again.

Nick
I think I understand, yet—

Iris
following him with her eyes
Red said he'd marry me, but I couldn't. I didn't love him.
I <u>don't</u> love him.

Nick stops, turns back, faces her.

Nick
But you're there. With him—

Iris
calmly
I told you it was involved.

*Nick goes to driver's side, gets in. Iris looks out at the
cemetery.*

Iris
Red said he'd take care of me, see me through the birth. I
couldn't go home—

She gets into the passenger's seat, glances at Nick.

Iris
You know my mom. She would have gone out of her
mind!

Nick nods, she looks away again.

Iris
So that's what I did. I stayed with him. And now—Steve's
almost grown.

Iris closes her eyes, a tear rolls down her cheek.

Iris
It's been long, and some of it has been ugly, but that's what I did.

Nick
You could've told me. I—

Iris
eyes open, she sniffles
I wrote you. A long letter, explaining everything.

Nick
stares at her, frowns
But I never got—

Iris
I know. I never mailed it. I still have it. It's all stamped and everything, ready to go.

Iris covers her mouth with her hand. Tears flow.

Iris
head bowed
I couldn't mail it. I was so ashamed. So awfully ashamed.

That night, in Miami, Bennie sits at the reporter's table. He reports to Alderman Emrin in Chicago by long distance.

Bennie
into phone
Guess what? Damon Runyon's here, covering the mayor.

Emrin
in Chicago
Runyon? Why would I—

Bennie
You know, he's the famous New York guy—

Emrin
Bennie, this is Chicago, not New York. I don't give a rat's rump about who's there from New York. How's the mayor?

Bennie
Oh. Sure. Nothing yet from Doctor Tice. But Woodard says he's critical.

Emrin
The mayor's critical? Wait. Who's Woodard? He's not on the list.

Bennie
He's the hospital superintendent.

A Nurse's Aide comes up to Bennie with a sheaf of papers. She hands Bennie one paper.

Bennie
distracted, looks at paper
Wait—

Emrin
That's funny. Woodard's not on my list.

Bennie scans the mimeographed copy.

Bennie
I just got handed Tice's report.
reading aloud
"Physicians still were optimistic yesterday but last night gangrene appeared in the right lung and—"

Emrin
Oh-oh.

Bennie
still reading aloud
"A third blood transfusion was performed today in an attempt to save his life and an attempt to check the gangrene was made, but the mayor did not respond."

Bennie
Oh—this don't sound good.
reading aloud
"He has lapsed into a coma and physicians say death is a matter of hours."

Emrin
Then there's no hope.

Bennie
Pretty gruesome. But that's what it says.

Emrin
Well, there's not much to do except wait. You be sure to—

Bennie
I'll call. As soon as there's word.

Meanwhile at Nick's flat in Chicago, Nick and Iris are seated at the small kitchen table after eating. Iris talks as Nick rises to clear the table.

Iris
—even though he's almost nineteen. I'll show you what I mean.

She opens her purse, reaches into it.

Iris
A couple days ago I said our fry pan was shot. 'Here, Mom,' he said, 'take this.' He handed me this.

She removes folded currency and lays them out, one by one.

Iris
Here's ten, twenty, twenty-five—

Nick
You don't know where he—?

Iris
He said, 'buy everything you need.' I asked him where it came from. He just smiled. 'Don't worry, Mom, it's easy money,' he said.

Nick removes bowls and plates from the table, places them in the sink.

Nick
So you think it was stolen. Is that—?

Iris
I know my son. Of course he stole the money. Or they pawned things.

shakes head
His father taught him how.

Iris's head sinks, her hands envelop her face.

Iris
suddenly overcome
Oh God! And now there's killing! What am I going to do? What?

Nick goes to her. She's near tears. He caresses her shoulders.

Nick
softly
Right now, I'm afraid there isn't anything you can do.

His comforting seems to calm her. She nods, pats his hand with hers. Nick returns to the table, gathers the silver.

Iris
Wait, Nick. I'll take care of that.

Nick
I'm used to it. It's nothing.

Iris gets up, helps Nick clear items from the table. She glances at the clock.

Iris
surprised
Oh God, it's late.

Nick is at the sink, his back to her. She approaches him, touches his upper arm gently.

Iris
I'm still shaky. But you got me away from there. Bless you, Nick, I'll never be able to thank you enough.

She goes to the table, picks up her purse.

Iris
Now I should go.

He turns to face her.

Nick
What?

Iris
Will you take me back—to the house?

Nick
gestures with both hands
No, Iris. You can't go back there. You'd be risking your life!

Iris
I don't know what else to do.

Nick
You've got to stay here.

Iris
What about Connie, your wife?

Nick
She's gone. We're separated—like I told you, she wants a different life.

Iris turns away, steps across the kitchen. There, she stops and faces him with moist eyes.

Iris
I appreciate the offer, Nick. But I don't have my—God, this is so awkward—

Nick holds the sink stopper in his hand.

Nick
I know—

He gestures with it.

Nick
awkwardly
We're both—kind of in the middle—

Iris
vague smile
More like a muddle.

They both chuckle, nervously. Iris returns her purse to her chair and goes to Nick. She takes the stopper from Nick, puts it in the drain, and turns on the faucet. Nick puts his arms lightly around her. She smiles, turns, looks into his eyes. They kiss, tentative at first, then with passion. As the splashing sound grows louder, Iris reaches behind her for the faucet handle but fails to grasp it.

Iris
pushing away
The water, Nick!

Without taking his eyes from her, he reaches and shuts the water off.

Nick
I love you Iris. I don't care if it is a muddle.

He embraces her, passion rising.

Iris
Can't you wait?

Nick
Wait?

Iris
Till we turn in?

NICK
smiles
Then you'll stay.

She slips from Nick's arms and steps away.

Iris
Yes, despite everything that's wrong with the way this has
happened—with me inflicting myself on you—

Looking down, she shakes her head.

Iris
And despite my son, who needs me. More than ever—
now.

Looking up, and at Nick with moist eyes.

Iris
And despite Red, who will be very angry that I'm not
there.

Resigned, she approaches Nick.

Iris
    Despite everything.

Nick takes her in his arms. She cradles his shoulders loosely with her hands, looks at his face.

Iris
Did you think I'd forgotten that day in the Shabbona Woods? I've thought of it, relived it a thousand times. I wanted you so badly. But—

Nick
I can't wait. The bed's a mess—

They embrace, passionately.

IRIS
It doesn't matter, Nick, it doesn't matter.

On the street outside the house on Rhodes Ave., a Ford V-8 Police car slows and parks in front. In the dim light, a uniformed cop exits from driver's side and a man in topcoat and felt hat exits the passengers side. They march to the front door and the cop knocks on the door.

The porch light comes on and the front door opens part way. Vapor coming from the men's mouths shows they are talking with someone inside. The door opens wider and Red Nedders, hatless, emerges. He stands with his hand gripping door. The men talk more.

The man in the topcoat gestures with his hands and arms, occasionally pointing at neighbors' houses. Red and the cop listen, standing nearly motionless.

The cop turns, strolls off the porch and lingers in the front yard. The man in the topcoat talks, then stops. He doffs his hat to Red and joins the cop in the yard. Red re-enters the house and closes the door. The porch light goes out.

The man in the topcoat talks fervently as he and the cop go to the police car. Inside the car they talk some more. The headlights come on and the police car drives away.

In Indiana the next day, a sandy road cut between marsh grass and cattails leads to a sandy parking lot. A lone Ford Model-T with "Porter Co. Sheriff" on its side is parked there. Inside, at a beat-up desk, Deputy Sheriff Frank talks on the phone.

Deputy Frank
into phone
We wouldn't have no responsibility for that car—seein's how it's on private property. Your—
pause
Your foreman jimmied the door?
pause
Oh. Okay. The door was already jimmied. He just opened it and—
pause
A dead body?
pause
A rolled-up rug. But what makes him think there's a dead body inside the rug?

pause
I understand. He didn't see a body, just—
pause
Didn't need to see anything. Just smelled it. A dead body.
pause
Yeah, I got it. We'll go take a look. It's probably just a dead cat.

In Chicago, inside the house on S. Rhodes Ave., Red Nedders stands, talks on the candlestick phone. Terry, swarthy and thirtyish, rocks in a rocking chair, smoking.

Red
into phone
How'd you get this number?
pause
Well, spit it out.

Terry
to Red
Who's that?

Red
into phone
Yeah? Carney? Who's Carney?

Terry stops rocking, yanks cigarette from his mouth.

Terry
Wait a minute. Who's—

Red clamps his hand over the mouthpiece.

Red

to Terry

Shut up! Might be on to something here.

into phone

I don't know what you're talking about.

pause

Yeah. What about it?

Terry gets up, approaches Red. Red backs away.

Red

into phone

Well, maybe. Maybe I might know about it.

Terry leans in, tries to hear what caller says. Red, excited, clamps his hand over the mouthpiece.

Red

to Terry

Get away! This sounds like the guy!

Terry smiles, backs away, smokes furiously.

Red

into phone

Yeah, I'm listening, but I don't know you—what's your—

pause

Okay. Okay. How much money we talking?

disappointed

Ah, you're a mug.

Terry, irritated, smashes his cigarette into the ashtray.

Terry

String him along! C'mon—

Red clamps his hand over the mouthpiece.

Red
to Terry
Shut up! I know! I know!
into phone
Yeah. Maybe we can. But the price is fifteen—

Terry grabs Red by the arm, thrusts two fingers at him.

Terry
No! Make it two. Two gees!

Red
firmly, into phone
Two gees. Yeah. That's it.
pause
Yeah, well, you was lowballing me.
pause
So what? Tell your man two thousand, or he can—

Terry
Don't let him—

Red
into phone
No way.

Red clamps his hand over the mouthpiece, turns to Terry.

Red
When?

Terry
What?

Red shakes the phone up and down for emphasis.

Red
to Terry
Christ-a-mighty! When?! Trade the goods for the
money—

Terry
Oh. Tell him small bills only, nothing over twenties.
And—

*His hand still over the mouthpiece, Red stomps his feet,
glares at Terry.*

Red
to Terry
When, dummy, when? And where?

Red removes his hand, reassures caller.

Red
into phone
Yeah, yeah. I'm thinking.
pause
No, there's nobody here but me.

Terry whispers to Red.

Terry
Tomorrow. Tomorrow night.

Red
into phone
Tomorrow. Midnight. Yeah.
pause
But nothing bigger than twenties. That's right.

pause
Call back tonight at six and I'll tell you where to meet.

In a Miami hotel lobby, Bennie faces the registration counter. He's in a rumpled suit, and next to him on the floor is his suitcase, his straw hat on top.

A forty-ish female clerk faces Bennie. It's 8:25 in the morning.

Bennie
Well, yeah. Here's the problem. I was supposed to be on that train last night.

Clerk
smiling
The special with the dignitaries and all?

Bennie
The funeral train, yeah. Poor Mayor Cermak—I'll miss him.
grins
Of course, I'm no dignitary.

Clerk
You missed the train?

Bennie
sheepish
No. Well, not exactly. See, they took reporters on there, so they could—you know—report.

Clerk
Sure thing.

Bennie

But I ain't no reporter.

laughs

I guess you're wondering what I am, really, eh?

The clerk smiles, knowingly.

Bennie

Just a guy needing a little break. And you—my, you have such a pretty smile!

Clerk

feigning concern

You said you had a problem. Maybe I can help. What is it?

Bennie

Well, I bought my ticket for today's train to Chicago. But this bill for the room—it's bigger than I figured.

Clerk

You're checking out, but you don't have cash for the bill. Is that it?

Bennie

Yeah, I'm kinda in a bind. The office was supposed to wire the money, but—

Clerk

We can take your personal check.

Bennie

Heh. That wouldn't be much help.

Clerk
How about giving me the name of your office. That would be in Chicago, right? If I contact them—

Bennie
defeated
No. No, that wouldn't be a good thing. Uh, no, let me double-check, maybe I miscounted—

Bennie grabs his hat, claps it on his head, smiles. He stoops, picks up the suitcase.

Bennie
pointing
I'll just step over there, by that table. I'll be right back. And, uh, thanks for all your help.

In his Chicago bank, Danny Hinkley sits in a wooden swivel chair behind a fancy wood desk with a nameplate that says "President." He faces the rear of the line of tellers, and talks quietly on the phone.

Hinkley
into phone
Two thousand! That's outrageous. I won't pay it.
trying to control his anger
Tell them it's outrageous.
pause
Yes, Zetner, I heard. You needn't remind me of the arithmetic.
pause
Yes, I understand you're sure. It's just the outrageousness of this—

After another pause, Hinkley sighs, looks up at the ceiling.

Hinkley
into phone
Alright. I'll arrange it. Goodbye, Zetner.

*At the 12th Avenue railroad station, a light drizzle keeps
the crowd bundled-up. Police are everywhere. Liver Jack in
his rumpled hat and overcoat approaches from the street and
joins the crowd.*
*A seven-car train, in black and purple bunting, rolls to a
stop. The locomotive, belching steam, tolls its bell. Family,
relatives and dignitaries disembark and are greeted by
Chicago officials.*

*Police clear a way through the throng as Mayor Cermak's
bronze casket, with a city flag, is hoisted from the single
baggage car and carried to a waiting hearse by pall bearers.*

*There are cries of grief as flashbulbs pop, news cameras snap,
and movie cameras whir.*

*When the procession is fully assembled, the hearse moves
slowly out of the station and north onto Michigan Avenue,
where thousands of mourners line the streets to pay their
respects.*

*Magazines and newspapers line the displays in the "Tobacco
and News" stand, not too far from Nick's flat. Nick stands
over a newspaper with the headline "JAP ARMIES SWEEP
CHINA." He glances outside at the drizzle, then resumes*

reading the story below the headline. The friendly newsdealer speaks to him.

Newsdealer
smiles
You planning on buying that paper?

Nick
Soon as I inherit enough to afford it.

The newsdealer shakes his head. Liver Jack, in his wet, rumpled hat and coat, enters. The newsdealer recognizes him and thumbs toward Nick.

Newsdealer
to Liver Jack
I should ask him for his library card.

Liver Jack
Aw, shut up.

Nick swivels to see Liver Jack, who shakes water from his sleeves.

Nick
to Liver Jack
Who bit you?

Liver Jack
This weather!
to newsdealer
Too bad this place can't afford some heat.
to Nick
At least the mayor's on his way home now.

Nick
Lotta people at the station?

Liver Jack
Me, the rest of the ward, and half of Chicago.

Liver Jack takes off his hat, shakes water from it.

Liver Jack
Not Sis, though. She's gone.

Nick
keenly
What d'you mean?

Liver Jack
We didn't want t'worry you. But—
low voice
your wife's left. Took her stuff, lock, stock and barrel.

Nick
Moved out?

Liver Jack tries to smooth his hat, maintains a low voice.

Liver Jack
You might as well know. She went off with Rich. Plays
with—whatsis name. Eddie Congrin?

Nick
Oh, Eddie Condon. The band. Rich? Rich who?

Liver Jack
Oh hell. Rich something. I wanted to kick him in the
balls so bad I can't remember his name.

Nick stares at the rainwater dripping outside.

Nick
It's okay. Maybe she'll be happier.

Liver Jack
Don't say that—I was planning to partake in your grief.

Liver Jack slaps his hat on his head, wraps his arm around Nick's shoulders.

Liver Jack
C'mon with me to "Kelly O's." We gotta drown your sorrows.

It's late, approaching midnight, in Nick's front room. Alone, he draws bills from stacks of fives, tens and twenties and stuffs them into a brown paper bag. When the money—$2,000—is in the bag, he dons his overcoat and hat and leaves out the front door with the bag. At his car, he opens the door, puts the bag on the floorboards, climbs behind the wheel.

Under streetlights, Nick drives deserted city streets, passing the Great A and P Tea store and other darkened businesses. Nick squints, looking left as he drives. He slows, focuses on each parked car facing him as he drives along the street.

Walgreen's is next on the right. There, a taxi and a police car are parked with headlights out. Light from the drugstore's neon sign reveals a uniformed cop inside the police car and a second cop who leans into the driver's open window of the taxi, talking with the cabbie. The cabbie laughs, stops to notice Nick's car as it passes, then laughs again. Neither cop pays attention to Nick's car.

He passes a park lit only by streetlamps. People covered with newspapers and folded out magazines sleep on benches. In the interior of the park, clumps of homeless men gather around a blazing barrel, flames licking upward. There's almost no traffic until a car with at young couple heads toward him. With his hand, Nick shields his eyes from the glare of oncoming headlights. The couple's car passes by, and Nick resumes, checking cars parked on the opposite curb.

Nearing an intersection, Nick slows. He cranks down the window and signals for a left turn. He turns left, then signals again and turns left at the next intersection. After closing the window, he cups his left hand to his mouth, warms it by blowing on it.

Nick passes a dimly-lit industrial neighborhood. At the Rapid Transit shops, idle rail cars occupy rails and switches. No autos are parked here, so he speeds up. Further along is a commercial section, where retail stores are shuttered and dark. Nick slows as he passes some cars parked on the opposite curb.

Following another arm signal, Nick's car turns left at an intersection, then left again at the following intersection. He retraces the starting street, again passing the Great A and P Tea store and Walgreen's. The taxi is the only car now parked at the curb. Its window is closed, the cabbie probably asleep.

As Nick repeats the circuit, awaiting a signal, he passes the park and the industrial neighborhood without incident. Then, as he enters the commercial section, he sees, a hundred yards ahead on the opposite curb, headlights of a sedan blink on-and-off quickly, three times.

He slows, pulls to the curb. Ahead, parked at the curb, is a small coupe, the only car parked nearby on his side of the street. The sedan is parked across the street, facing him, about thirty yards distant. Nick stops a few yards behind the coupe, sets his hand brake, turns off his headlights.

Now under a streetlamp, Nick shifts his car to neutral, rolls down his window. All is silent except for the throb of his motor. Nick stares at the sedan across the street that blinked its headlights, but nothing stirs. After a couple of minutes, Nick opens his door, steps out, and lingers next to his car, behind his open door.

Time passes with no action. Nick edges outside the door, spreads his arms and hands to show he's unarmed. The driver's door of the sedan across the street opens and a man steps out in overcoat and hat, brim pulled low. Trailing smoke from a cigarette, the man closes his door, jams his hands into his coat pockets and plants himself next to sedan with feet spread apart. It's Terry.

Abruptly, Nick hears the click of a car door and the driver's door of the coupe <u>ahead</u> of Nick springs open. A hatless Red alights. Just as he turns toward Nick, Nick sees a glint from something in Red's hand. He darts back behind his car door.

Red laughs, raises his hand with the pint bottle that caught the light, takes a couple of swallows, laughs again.

Red
Scared ya, huh?

Nick moves out from behind his door.

Nick
You didn't say you'd have two cars—and a gunner.

Red takes a couple of steps toward Nick, holds out his free hand.

Red
You take me for a dummy? Let's see the cash.

Nick
You'll get it when I see the goods. Tell the gunner to air out his hands.

Red screws the lid onto his bottle, waves to Terry. Terry withdraws a hand, takes the cigarette from his mouth. A trail of smoke issues from his mouth. He withdraws the other hand. Nick steps out from behind his door.

Nick
Okay. Now—the goods.

Terry
to Red
Speed it up! Ain't got all night.

Red
to Terry
Keep your pants on!

Red stuffs the bottle in his pocket, reaches inside the coupe, pulls out an envelope, struts with it to Nick and hands it over.

Red
Ain't much.

Nick unwinds the string, opens it, counts and thumbs nine snapshots. He removes one photo, holds it under the light from the streetlamp, glances at it. He replaces the photo, closes the envelope and nods to Red.

Red
Gimme that! And get the money.

Nick hands envelope to Red, gets the sack of money from his car, hands it to Red.

Nick
Count it if you want.

Red grabs the sack, opens it. He pulls out a few wads of bills, selects one bill, waves it at Nick.

Red
What're you trying to pull? This is a goddamn five-dollar bill!

Nick
You said 'small bills only.' What'd you expect?

Red tosses the envelope to Nick, who catches it.

Red
Get out of here, you bastard.

Red turns and reenters his coupe with the sack of money. As Nick gets into his car with the envelope, Red's head emerges from his car's window. He yells back at Nick.

Red
What you waiting for? Sunrise?

Nick drives from the curb, passes Red's coupe and Terry's sedan, and travels down the street. He glances at the rearview mirror, sees Terry's sedan pull into the street. Then Red's coupe makes a U-turn in the street and follows after Terry's sedan. Their taillights dim into the distance.

It's the next day at Liver Jack's house. In the living room, Liver Jack selects a cigar from his small china humidor as Noddy enters.

Noddy
I'll go upstairs and tidy up.

Liver Jack
Now just a minute.

Noddy
Will you see if you can do something with your shaving materials?

Liver Jack
Now look. I'm not about to start living out of a shoe. And there's no need to 'tidy up.'

Liver Jack returns the cigar to the humidor.

Noddy
But they'll be here in a few minutes.

Liver Jack
So? Everything was good enough for Sis the way it was. I don't see putting ourselves out, even if it is for Nick.

Noddy
It's no bother. And I think I left that nice warm comforter in the—

Liver Jack
Fer crying out loud. It's not even noon. She's not going to want to go to bed the minute they walk in.

Noddy
Well, I distinctly remember putting the pillows away in the cedar chest.

Liver Jack pulls a cigar from the humidor.

Liver Jack
Okay. Okay. I give up.

He runs the cigar under his nose to smell it.

Liver Jack
But I draw the line at rearranging the bathroom. She can just—

Noddy points out the front window.

Noddy
interrupting
Oh look. That's Nick's car. They're here!

Liver Jack
Good. Nick's girl will just have to figure out—on her own—how to survive living here. Now answer the door.

119

At the Porter County, Indiana Sheriff's office, Deputy Frank sits at his desk. Smartly dressed in suit and tie, Federal Agent Harris stands and explains the day's operations.

Agent Harris
Now that Mrs. Sossek has identified the body, Agent Bingham and I are going out to South Shore Acres to print the car.

Deputy Frank
has no idea
Uh-huh.

Agent Harris
I'm betting the perpetrator or perpetrators left prints somewhere on it. And we'll package up that rug. Then we'll get the Olds towed to the Chicago Impound Lot—

Deputy Frank
Sounds like the Bureau keeps you guys pretty busy.

Agent Harris
smiles
We try to keep Mr. Hoover happy.

Nick opens his front door and Liver Jack, in coat and hat, enters the front room.

Liver Jack
Ah, the streets. Terrible.

Nick
Icy?

Liver Jack sheds hat and coat, Nick takes them.

Liver Jack
No. The procession. They took Cermak from his home to
City Hall. I couldn't even get—say!
alarmed, sniffs air
you got something burning—

Nick
Huh? Oh, yeah. Had a little bonfire. It's out now.

Liver Jack
Glad it ain't your coffeecake.
smiles
You'd break your teeth on the raisins if it was.

Nick
C'mon into the kitchen. I'll get some coffee.

*They go into the kitchen and Liver Jack sits at the table. As
he talks, Nick pours coffee, returns the coffeepot to the stove.*

Nick
—he asked if I had all the snaps, I said I had nine. He
asked if I had an ashtray. I didn't get it—

Liver Jack
laughs
How was you to know he wanted you to burn 'em?
turning serious
So now you're a rich man.

Nick
You mean the reward—yeah, soon.

Liver Jack frowns at his coffee cup.

Nick
Sorry, I don't have any cream.

Liver Jack
He didn't deliver the money?

Nick
sits
It's coming by courier, he said.

Liver Jack
Well, if Connie divorces you, you and Iris can get married and live happy ever after.

Nick
Not really. Finding the body made the papers yesterday. When they figure who it is, they'll trace it to the house on Rhodes. Iris will be in hot water.

Nick gets up, takes the coffee pot.

Liver Jack
But she didn't—you said she was at the market when Sossek got killed.

Nick
She's lived there a long time! The neighbors know her! The cops might be looking for her right now.

Nick adds coffee to his cup, tips pot toward Liver Jack.

Nick
More?

Liver Jack
shakes head

It don't seem right.

Nick returns pot to stove.

Nick
I'm really worried—she could be arrested. That Red, he's a real bum. If they catch him, I wouldn't put it past him to involve her.

Liver Jack
gestures
Look, Nick. I got a certain pull, in the ward—maybe downtown. But I don't know how I can help—

Nick
I think she's gotta disappear. Get out of Chicago. Far away.

Nick starts to drink, pauses with the cup in the air.

Nick
What d'you think about Canada?

Liver Jack
Well, let's see. Get her to Detroit, then—cross at Windsor?

Nick sets his cup down, shakes his head.

Nick
Too dangerous. They'd be on the lookout.

Nick
Say, I know. How about a boat? It could take her straight across to Ontario—

A military knock on the front door interrupts. Nick gets up to answer.

Liver Jack
Nah. The upper lake's frozen over.

Nick goes to the front room, opens the front door, faces a man in jodhpurs, high boots, jacket with many buttons, Sam Browne belt with leather-covered holster. He's from Brink's.

Brinks Man
Delivery for Mr. Nicholas Zetner.

Nick
Uh—that's me.

Brinks Man
Okay. Thank you. I'll be right back.

He turns to leave and Nick closes the door.

Liver Jack
from the kitchen
Who's there?

Nick
It's a delivery. Must be—

Liver Jack enters from the kitchen, spreads his hands.

Liver Jack
So where's the delivery guy?

Nick
He went to get it—

He peeks out the door, sees the Brink's man.

Nick
Here he is.

The Brinks man enters, carrying a neat, string-tied bundle and a form pad. He gives Nick a fountain pen and thrusts the form pad at Nick.

Brinks Man
Sign right here.

The delivery form, in fancy print says, "Brinks Express Co. Delivery Receipt." Below is a handwritten message: "Washington Park Bank to Nicholas Zetner—D.H." Nick signs it, hands it and pen to the Brinks man. The Brinks man hands the bundle to Nick, retreats and leaves out the door. Nick loosens the string on the bundle.

Liver Jack
This I gotta see.

Nick tears at the bundle, exposing packets of currency wrapped in double rubber bands.

Later, in the kitchen, Nick sits at the table. It is stacked with packets of small bills. Liver Jack stands next to the table in his coat, hat in one hand.

Liver Jack
I've been thinking.

Nick
Not investments, I hope.

Liver Jack
No. How to get to Canada. But I gotta go.

He slaps his hat on his head.

Nick
You've got an idea?

Liver Jack
Now that you got all that money, there's a guy I know. Runs "Greengold Deliveries" out of Green Bay.

Nick
Green Bay? How would—

Liver Jack buttons his coat, turns to leave.

Liver Jack
Lemme see if I can get ahold of him.

Before dawn, a uniformed policeman (Porterman) is behind the wheel of a car parked on S. Rhodes Avenue in Chicago. Detective Kolmser, in the passenger seat, lights a match to see his watch, which shows a few minutes before four a.m.

Kolmser
Damned radium dials don't work worth a shit.

Kolmser blows out the match, scans the target house.

Kolmser
There's a coupe parked in the drive. Probably Nedder's. Let's go.

The two men quietly exit the car, mount the front porch of the house. Kolmser pounds on the front door.

Kolmser
to house
Chicago Police! Bureau of Detectives. Open up!

No action, inside the house or out.

Kolmser
louder
We got a warrant! Open up!

A dog begins barking.

Kolmser
looking to his left
Oh great. Indoors?

Porterman
Nope. Backyard.

Porterman tiptoes left. The barking grows louder, more ferocious.

Porterman
It ain't coming. Must be chained.

Kolmser
Nobody's answering.

Kolmser gestures towards his right.

Kolmser
Go around there. See.

Porterman gropes his way off the right side of porch and around the driveway side of the house.

Kolmser waits.

Porterman
returning
Side door's unlocked.

Kolmser quickly follows Porterman around the right side of the house as the dog continues to bark.

Inside the house's vestibule, Porterman, with gun drawn, has switched on the lights. Kolmser enters through the outside door, gestures for Porterman to go into the next room (kitchen).

Lights come on in the neighbor's house next door on the left. The dog continues to bark, and from somewhere inside, we hear the dog's master.

Neighbor
to dog
Foster! Shut up!

Kolmser comes around from the driveway side, circles past the coupe, and enters the back yard. The dog's bark changes to a growl.

Kolmser
toward the alley
Morgan! See anything?

The dog's growl changes to a vicious snarl. In the cinder alley, Morgan, in plain clothes, stands behind two trash cans.

Morgan
Nothing.

Neighbor
to dog
Foster! Shut up!

Morgan
to the neighbor
Can't you shut that mutt up?

Neighbor
Who's that?

Kolmser climbs onto the back porch, directs his voice over the solid fence separating the two lots.

Kolmser
to the neighbor
It's the police, sir. Chicago Police. You seen Mr. Nedders?

The dog snarls fiercely.

Neighbor
How should I know?

From the neighbor's we hear a door slam followed by a screen door that bangs.

Neighbor
outside, to dog
There boy. There. There.

The dog stops snarling, whimpers.

It's dawn. The scene lightens as Kolmser talks to Porterman in the kitchen of the target house.

Kolmser
I don't see much, but don't touch nothing. I'll call in, get help going through everything.

Porterman
What about that window?

Kolmser
What window?

Porterman
That window upstairs. Wide open.

Kolmser
Yeah. Kinda strange. Wide open like that, furnace churning full tilt. I dunno.

Nick the Magician (Patrick McHenry-Kroetch)*

Grip Josh Wallace suggests lighting setup. (l. to r.) Wes Deitrick, Jesse James Hennessy, and May Deitrick

Speakeasy patron (Jason Young)

Nick (Patrick McHenry-Kroetch) weighs his options*

Iris (Amy Sherman)

Director Jesse James Hennessy

Nick discovers Iris at speakeasy
(Patrick McHenry-Kroetch, Amy Sherman*

Directors plan scene as Production Assistant looks on.
(l. to r.) May Deitrick, Jesse James Hennessy,
Wes Deitrick

Nick confronts Iris (Patrick McHenry-Kroetch,
Amy Sherman)*

Photos with asterisk (*) from film footage, Jade
Warpenburg, Director of Photography. All other photos
courtesy John Austin, www.austinspace.com.

Act III

Outside a hangar at Chicago's Municipal Airfield, Nick looks at a yellow, high-winged airplane. Its motor is in the nose, with a large 2-blade propeller. On the plane's side is "GREENGOLD DELIVERIES, GREEN BAY, WIS."

Ed "Crackup" Mackison, a chubby man in horsehide flying jacket and canvas helmet with rolled up earflaps, explains to Nick.

Crackup
Yeah, well, hardly nobody calls me Ed. That would have passed, but it was my very first solo. See I landed okay, and o'course the taxiways was just dirt—

When Nick leans his hand on the fabric-covered fuselage, it yields. Nick yanks his hand away.

Crackup
smiles
I'm taxiing along fine when the starboard wheel plunks into a big pothole. Well, that old Jenny whipped right around. The prop dug a neat ditch right across the taxiway.

Crackup laughs and draws the idea of a ditch with his hand. Nick glances at the plane.

Nick
Not this airplane—

Crackup
Oh no. The Jenny. But there was a lotta dust.
chuckles
   I ended up with a bloody nose, but the airplane was okay.

Nick, into the spirit of the story, smiles.

Crackup
You shoulda heard the guffaws from the hangar gallery. They laughed till they cried. Been known as 'Crackup' ever since.
soberly
So, you're friend of Liver Jack—

Nick
Nick. Guess he told you I'm looking to go to Canada.

Crackup
Just you, huh?

Nick
Two of us.

Crackup nods, yanks open the cockpit door.

Crackup
Yep. This here's the baby. 'Course I seldom fly there. Now and then, when somebody's desperate for a motor, a package or something.

Nick looks inside at the cramped cabin. Up front is a wicker seat for the pilot. Behind that are two side-by-side wicker seats for passengers. The seats are narrow, jammed to the cabin sides with no elbow space and little leg room.

Nick
Wow—not much room.

Crackup
It's a flyin machine, not the Twentieth Century Limited.
Okay for two ordinary-size people. But not much for
luggage. About what fits in a lunch bucket.

Nick
How soon could we leave?

Crackup
In a hurry, eh? Well, that depends on lotta things.
'Specially the weather. But it's fair for the next few days.

He points up at the wing, then at the wing on the other side.

Crackup
There's just the two tanks. Twenty-five gallons apiece.
That's about four-hundred miles, enough to get from
Green Bay across to Ontario.
smiles
With a quart or two left over.

Nick
From Green Bay?

Crackup
Oh sure. I'm just down to Chicago to pick up a
transmission for a tractor. We fly outa Green Bay.

Nick
So how much would it cost—for two people to—
Ontario.

Crackup
You mean Sudbury and back?

Nick
One-way.

Crackup
Oh yeah, I see. Well, one-way or round-trip, it's no difference—the airplane hasta get home just the same. Usually I'd charge three thousand a person—

Nick
stunned
Whew. That's a lot more—

Crackup
Yeah, it's a lotta green. Heck, you could just take a bus to Detroit, the two of you. Cross at Windsor. If you wanted, that is.
pauses
Course you'd still have a long haul to Sudbury. Unless you were just interested in gettin across the—

Nick
No, No, we want to fly. It's just a lot of money, that's all.

Crackup
Look Nick. It costs on account of me.
points index finger at his forehead
Dead of winter, colder than a polar bear's behind. You're paying me to find that landing strip outside Sudbury with nothing but snow far's you can see.

He pauses to let that sink in.

Crackup

Then I gotta hope my man with the hand crank can fill my tanks so I got gas for the trip back. But you're a friend of Jack's—I'll make you a deal. Five-thousand for the two of you.

Crackup and Nick have moved inside the hangar. Crackup sits next to a dirty workbench with airplane parts on it. He hands Nick two yellow scarves.

Crackup

You two take the train tomorrow night. Get off in Green Bay wearing these. Yolanda picks you up, takes you to the airfield the next morning. Now, listen careful—

Crackup stands, makes points jabbing his finger into the opposite palm.

Crackup

It's four hours in the air. Dress warm, stocking cap, mittens—no gloves, your fingers'll freeze. Don't drink nothing for six hours before takeoff—you can't pee up there.
pauses
One more thing. Bring two paper bags, line 'em with plenty of wax paper. That's for you to toss your cookies in.
pauses again
You got that?

Nick

I—I understand.

Crackup
Yolanda don't make change, and she don't do deals. So make sure you come with the five-thousand, even, in cash.

On Chicago's north side, trailing parts of Cermak's funeral procession—marchers, cars with funeral flags—pass slowly behind a wood barricade that blocks the intersection. Liver Jack, in his car, approaches the barricade and stops. A traffic cop behind the barricade gestures for Liver Jack to turn around. Liver Jack's car backs into an alley, turns around and drives off.

Liver Jack enters a heavily-parked street. He finds one empty space, parks, exits the car, charges down the street on the sidewalk.

Liver Jack arrives, puffing, at the Bohemian National Cemetery with the ceremony in progress.

Standing throngs surround the Cermak mausoleum. His flag-draped casket sits in front on velvet, surrounded by flower decorations. Uniformed police flank seated dignitaries. In a roped-off, carpeted area, Cermak's three daughters sit, weeping.

A Mason reads an eulogy. Nearby are hundreds of Bohemian Odd Fellows in red or blue ornate collars trimmed in gold and Bohemian Orphanage children holding white flowers.

Liver Jack stands at the edge of the huge crowd. He blows on his hands to warm them.

In front of the mausoleum, a boy speaks Czech in a tribute to Cermak's support of the Bohemian Orphanage. After a brief nondenominational blessing, the American Legion honor guard fires a rifle salute. A bugler blows taps.

In the bedroom at Nick's flat, two yellow scarves and other clothing litter the bed—two stocking caps, several pairs of gloves, a woolen coat and a sheepskin coat. Nick digs into bottom of the closet, pulls out two pair of mittens. As he inspects them and tosses them onto bed, he hears sounds of a commotion followed by a weak tapping noise. He stops, glares at the doorway and goes to the front room where he opens the front door enough to peer out.

Outside is a lanky eighteen-year-old in a flannel shirt that's half untucked and trousers with dirty knees. The boy stands there, gripping his left elbow.

Steve
Uh. Mr. Zetner?

Nick
Yeah. What do you want?

Steve
shivers
I—I'm Steve. Can I—

Nick widens the opening.

Nick
What! You're—Iris's boy?

Steve
teeth chatter
Mom said you'd—maybe you'd—

With door open, Nick motions Steve inside.

Nick
points
Get in here, kid. Sit there.

Nick closes the door. Steve sits, shaking with purple lips, messy clothes, mussed hair. He rubs his hands over his body trying to warm himself. His torn sleeve shifts, showing a bloody, skinned left forearm and elbow.

Nick
What're you doing here?

Steve
shivers
So cold.

Nick
Yeah, wait. I'll get you something—

Nick goes to bedroom, returns with a woolen coat, spreads it across Steve's body.

Nick
What happened? How'd you get here?

Steve
straining

Nowhere to go. Freezing my ass off. Mom told me—
where you live.

Nick
gestures
No coat, no hat, no wonder. What's going on?

*Skinned knuckles show as Steve lifts the coat, brushes dirt
from a knee with his free hand.*

Steve
I know. I don't have no right.
starts to get up
I'll leave.

Nick
raises his hand
Sit still. I just want to know what's going on.

Steve allows the coat to cover him again.

Steve
I had to get out. Away.

Nick
Away—from the house—on Rhodes?

Steve nods.

Nick
Why?

Steve
looks down
Cops. Cops pounded on the door. Hollered about a
warrant or something.

Nick
So?

Steve
I ducked out the upstairs window—onto the roof—slid down—

Nick
Oh. You were trying to escape. Because of Sossek?

Steve nods slowly, then looks at Nick.

Steve
surprised
Oh, you know.

Nick
What about your dad?

Steve
resigned
I guess you know everything.

Nick
Did your dad get away, too?

Steve
He was already gone. I dropped into the neighbor's yard, but I didn't see him. Maybe he saw the cops—drive up.

Steve, now warmer, glances around. He lifts the coat, lays it aside.

Steve
rises
I don't think I should be here. I better go.

Nick
blocking his way
Just a minute, Steve. I know you're trying to protect your dad. According to the paper, he's wanted for murder.

Steve
disbelieving
Murder?!

Nick
Did he kill Carney Sossek?

Steve sinks slowly back into the chair.

Steve
It wasn't murder. There was a big argument, a fight, but—

Nick
Wait. If there's a fight, it's okay to kill?

Steve abruptly shivers. He grabs the coat, covers himself again.

Steve
hedges
Well—

Nick
The two of you carted off the body. You think that's okay?

Steve
I didn't say that. But Dad said we had to, to get rid of it, to protect Mom.

Nick turns, takes a step, turns back, faces Steve.

Nick
Your mom's right. You think if your dad tells you something's okay, it's okay. It's not. Now your mom's in real danger—

Steve
concerned
You mean because—

Nick
Yeah, because of you, because of what you and Red—

Steve
But we had to—

Nick
firmly
No you didn't. Killing's wrong. You knew that. Everything you did was wrong.

Steve lowers his head, looks away.

Nick
Well, wasn't it?

Steve shrugs his shoulders. He finally answers, his voice clogged.

Steve
near tears
Yeah. I guess.

Nick
scolds
You guess? You know. You know because your mother—
your mother who suffered almost every day to raise
you right—your mother who loves you more than
anything—your mother, she taught you right from
wrong. <u>Didn't</u> she?

A tear rolls down Steve's cheek. He wipes it away.

Steve
I—I wasn't looking at that.

Nick
quietly now
You saw it. But you followed your dad. Like a little boy.
Now you see how that's turned out.

Steve
shakes his head
Yeah—I wish—

Nick
You're not a little boy any more, Steve. You're almost a
man.

Steve
slowly, contrite
I know. I wish I could—

Nick
sadly
Sure you do, Steve. And if wishes were Duesenbergs, we'd
all drive Michigan Avenue—in style.

At the Police Station, Detective Kolmser sits at his wooden desk. A smoldering stub rests in his ashtray. Black burn scars surround it. Kolmser reads a file through ill-fitting reading glasses. Sitting facing him—in handcuffs—is Red Nedders, dressed only in a lightweight shirt and string-tied pajama bottoms.

Kolmser
Says here Mrs. Sossek positively identified her husband's body.

Kolmser eyes Red over the top of the glasses.

Kolmser
waves paper
This here goes to the prosecutor, who'll try to get a grand jury—

Red stares at, and wiggles the toes of his bare feet.

Red
Ain't you got any heat in this place?

Kolmser
It's about like this in the wintertime.

Kolmser removes and holds his eyeglasses in his hand.

Kolmser
'Course you're not exactly dressed for February in Chicago.

Red
defensive
I just went out for a breath of air.

Kolmser
Eight blocks from your house?

Red
Least you could do is get me a blanket.

Kolmser returns eyeglasses to his nose, looks at the file.

Kolmser
The prosecutor will seek a true bill, naming you—

Red tries to gesture, but the handcuffs hinder.

Red
It ain't illegal to be on the street, is it?

Kolmser, irritated, drops the file to the desk, whips off his glasses.

Kolmser
What'd ya run for, then? And try to hide behind the grocery store?

Red
nods toward ashtray
You ever smoke that thing? Seems like it's the only heat going here.

Kolmser returns glasses to his nose, searches file.

Kolmser
Where's the lady—uh—

Kolmser
adjusts glasses
Name's 'Iris.' Where's she?

Red
eyes still on the ashtray
You ain't gonna smoke it, you could let me have a puff.

Kolmser
I asked you a question.

Red
And I told you, I didn't kill nobody. I was just walking around. You got me all wrong.

Kolmser
That's not what the warrant says.

Kolmser slaps the file closed, starts to get up.

Kolmser
You're heading down to the Dearborn Street jail.

Red
Yeah, well. Leastwise maybe they'll have some heat down there.

Inside the noisy, cavern-like lobby of the railway terminal in Chicago are ticket windows, a telegraph office, a lunch room, the station master's office. Passengers enter and leave through distant openings onto downtown streets with cab stands and auto traffic. Baggage men corral suitcases, clerks rush about with carts of U.S. Mail and passengers, many with luggage, climb and descend the staircase to the waiting room upstairs.

Nick and Steve stand, in coats, on the third step of the staircase, scanning the crowd. Iris and Liver Jack have just entered the lobby. Steve abruptly drops the cloth bag he carries and rushes toward Iris. She sees Steve and hurries toward him. Mother and son joyously embrace.

Nick follows after Steve with the bag. He drops the bag near the embracing couple and throws his arms around them. Liver Jack stands aside, perplexed.

Liver Jack
grasps Nick's arm, nods toward Steve
I brought her, like you said. Who's this?

Nick
He's Iris's son.
to Steve
Steve, meet Jack Horn.

Steve awkwardly takes Liver Jack's hand. Iris throws herself into Nick's arms, they kiss, slowly separate.

Iris
to Nick
What's going on? Why are we—

Nick
to Iris and Jack
I'll explain. But first—

Nick digs in the bag, pulls out the sheepskin coat. Iris sheds her cloth coat and he helps her into the sheepskin.

Iris
Ooh! It's so warm—feels good!

Nick picks up the bag, turns toward the staircase.

Nick

C'mon upstairs. I'll explain while we wait.

The upstairs waiting room is crowded with passengers clogging the vast marble floor or sitting on long, wood benches. Nick, Iris, Steve and Liver Jack stand near one of the benches.

Nick
to Iris and Jack
Steve and I rode the 'L,' took Madison to get down here. I bought tickets on the seven-ten, one-way to Green Bay.

Nick displays two tickets.

Nick
to Iris and Steve
These are the scarves you'll wear off the train so Mackison's wife Yolanda will recognize you.
digs in the bag, exposes yellow scarves
It'll be really cold flying, so I brought enough warm clothing for the two of you.

Iris
stunned
<u>Two</u> of us?! What about you?

Nick
flatly
There are only two seats on that airplane, Iris. One for you, one for Steve.

Nick hands tickets and bag to Steve.

Iris
realizes
You mean—two seats? But—

Nick
That's it. No more—

Iris
cutting him short
No—no! Earlier you said you and I would escape, together.

Nick
Yeah, I know. But that can't be. Steve needs to change his life. To change his life, he has to start over. He won't get that chance if he's here—on his own.

Iris
Oh Nick, I know what you're trying to do. But—no. I love you, I won't go. Not without you.
near tears, she turns away
I can't go without you.

Nick lightly grasps her shoulders.

Nick
sharply
You can't stay here. There may be a warrant out for you right now. They'll call it 'accessory to a felony.' Or worse.

She turns around, looks directly at him, tears streaming.

Iris
But I didn't do anything. They can't blame me for something I didn't do.

Nick

Neighbors saw you, day in, day out, for years, there on Rhodes Avenue. The D.A. will call them as witnesses. There's no other choice.

Liver Jack puffs hard on his cigar.

Iris
weeps
Our love, I can't just throw it away.

Nick
shakes head
No, never. I'm not giving that up—even if we're far apart.

Iris
pleads
But our plans—the two of us together in a new life—

He thumbs toward Steve.

Nick

If you and I leave, Steve's stuck here in Chicago, without help, without direction. Without someone who loves him—like you love him.

Steve looks down, fumbles with his jacket, looks at Iris.

Nick
to Iris
Without you, who can help him straighten out his life.

Nick leans close to her, lowers his voice.

Nick

How much do the police know?—about what happened?
If Steve stays here and he's arrested, you'd regret ever
leaving. Forever. You know you would.

Iris
reluctantly nods
I hate this. It's terrible.
She wipes tears with her hand.

Nick
One more thing.

He points at the bag, speaks quietly close to Iris's ear.

Nick
In there is a bundle of money. There's five thousand for
the flight. The rest will get you started in Sudbury. I love
you.

*Liver Jack, Nick, Iris and Steve enter one of the dimly-lit
platforms that divide the tracks in the train shed. They go to
the ticketed passenger car while vapor and gritty smoke issue
from its locomotive. Other passengers, loved ones and porters
hurry about.*

*Outside the car, Nick stands with his arm around Iris's
shoulders while Steve and Liver Jack linger nearby. Iris, face
wet with tears, glances at the car, turns to Nick, throws her
arms around his neck.*

Iris
I'll never forget what you're doing. But I can't take it—leaving you.

Nick
smiles
You are my love. Forever.
They kiss.

Down platform is the conductor.

Conductor
announces loudly
All aboard! For Waukegan, Kenosha, Milwaukee—points north.

Steve hoists the bag, clambers into the car's vestibule, turns around.

Steve
C'mon, Mom—I'll give you a hand.

Iris, clinging to Nick, shakes her head, tears streaming.

Iris
to Steve
A minute—
to Nick
I love you—I—I can't say goodbye.

The locomotive chugs, its bell clangs.

Nick grasps her wrists, breaks away.
Nick
You got to get aboard. The train's leaving—

The car lurches. Iris thrusts one arm toward Steve, who grasps it, helps her onto the step. The car begins to roll.

Iris
frantic
Oh, no!

Iris almost falls, Steve grabs her, helps her into the vestibule. A trainman on board closes the vestibule door and the train moves out, toward the end of the shed.

Nick moves down the platform, keeping pace with the train. Moving ever faster, he scans the windows for Iris, but the train quickly outruns him. He falls behind and finally stops.

The red lamp on the last car recedes as the train leaves the shed. Beyond and into the night, its whistle emits a faint, waning wail.

Nick and Liver Jack leave the train shed and enter the waiting room. They head for the staircase.

Liver Jack
concerned
You all right?

Nick walks straight ahead, lost in thought.

Liver Jack
Hey. Hey, Nick!

Nick
turns head to Liver Jack
Uh. Huh?

Liver Jack
You were a million miles away.

Nick
Maybe it's all an illusion.

Liver Jack chuckles.
Liver Jack
You been to too many magic shows.

The two men descend the stairs. At the lobby, they step off the stairs and walk toward the opening to the street.

Liver Jack puffs on his cigar, pulls it from his mouth.
Liver Jack
They all met over there at the Morrison, big confab.

Nick
Yeah?.

Liver Jack
Looks like the City Council will try to decide if they can vote on one of the members to replace Cermak.

Nick
So what about Ed Kelly, then?

Liver Jack
Word is, he's Pat Nash's guy. If the stars align and Lake Michigan don't turn to hog slop, that is.

He takes another puff, lets out a smoke trail.
Liver Jack
Then maybe I'll get to move up. Been a precinct captain for fourteen years now.

Nick
Swell. Put in a word for me. Maybe I could do some kind of show at the world's fair that's supposed to open.

Liver Jack stops walking. Nick stops also.

Liver Jack
Why work? You got a lotta money now, even after paying for the airplane and all, right?

Nick
shakes his head
Nope. Not a dime. Gave it all to Iris—so she could start a new life up there.

Liver Jack squints, does a big draw on his cigar.
Liver Jack
Hmm.

They walk to street-side and halt. Cars pass by them.

Nick
I figure, working for a salary for the city, I'd get a vacation.

Liver Jack
Maybe.

He yanks the cigar from his mouth.
Liver Jack
Suppose you got this here vacation, where'd you go?

Nick's gaze follows a car turning from one street onto the other.
Nick
Canada, probably.

Liver Jack rams the cigar back in his mouth, grins.
Liver Jack
Ha. Are you sure?

FADE OUT.

END

For more information or to contact the authors go to:

www.IllusionsOfMagic.com